学术顾问
（以姓氏笔画为序）

王　宏　冯智文　李正栓　李丽生　原一川

Academic Advisors

Wang Hong　Feng Zhiwen　Li Zhengshuan

Li Lisheng　Yuan Yichuan

主　编

李昌银

副主编

黄　瑛　彭庆华

General Editor

Li Changyin

Professor of English　Yunnan Normal University

Associate General Editors

Huang Ying

Professor of English　Yunnan Normal University

Peng Qinghua

Professor of English　Yunnan Normal University

云南少数民族经典作品英译文库

Classics of Yunnan Ethnic Groups in English Translation

主编　李昌银　General Editor　Li Changyin
副主编　黄瑛　彭庆华　Associate General Editors　Huang Ying & Peng Qinghua

Da-gu Da-leng Gelaibiao
达古达楞格莱标

编著◎芒市非物质文化遗产保护中心
英译◎杨慧芳
译校◎［美］包琼

Compiled by Intangible Cultural Heritage
Protection Center of Mangshi City
Translated into English by Yang Huifang
Revised by Joan Cecile Boulerice

云南出版集团
云南人民出版社

图书在版编目（CIP）数据

达古达楞格莱标：汉、英 / 芒市非物质文化遗产保护中心编著；杨慧芳英译. -- 昆明：云南人民出版社，2020.2

（云南少数民族经典作品英译文库 / 李昌银主编）

ISBN 978-7-222-19075-7

Ⅰ. ①达… Ⅱ. ①芒… ②杨… Ⅲ. ①德昂族—史诗—中国—汉、英 Ⅳ. ①I222.7

中国版本图书馆CIP数据核字(2020)第028258号

出 品 人	李　维　　赵石定
项目统筹	周　祥　　殷筱钊
项目组稿	郭木玉
责任编辑	郭木玉　　溥　思
装帧设计	马　滨　　石　斌
责任校对	明　珍　　王琳淇　　费　珺
责任印制	陆卫华　　代隆参

云南少数民族经典作品英译文库
Classics of Yunnan Ethnic Groups in English Translation

达古达楞格莱标
Da-gu Da-leng Gelaibiao

编著◎芒市非物质文化遗产保护中心
英译◎杨慧芳
译校◎[美]包琼

Compiled by Intangible Cultural Heritage Protection Center of Mangshi City
Translated into English by Yang Huifang
Revised by Joan Cecile Boulerice

出　版	云南出版集团　云南人民出版社
发　行	云南人民出版社
社　址	昆明市环城西路609号
邮　编	650034
网　址	www.ynpph.com.cn
E-mail	ynrms@sina.com
开　本	787mm×1092mm　1/16
印　张	17.75
字　数	242千
版　次	2020年2月第1版第1次印刷
印　刷	云南出版印刷集团有限责任公司　云南新华印刷一厂
书　号	ISBN 978-7-222-19075-7
定　价	105.00元

云南人民出版社
微信公众号

序 一

◎李正栓

民族典籍英译是传播中国文化、文学和文明的重要途径，是中华文化走出去的重要组成部分。文化与文学的传播，是一个国家提高文化软实力的重要方式，在文化交流和文明建设中起着不可或缺的作用，对提高国家对外话语权、构建国家对外话语体系以及对建设世界文学都有积极意义。

中国各少数民族拥有许多优秀的典籍，具有很高的文物价值、文学价值和文化价值。各民族的先人们通过口头流传或用文字记述了他们各具特色的文化。各少数民族几乎都有自己民族的创世史、史诗和神话传说。

中国民族典籍独具特色，不可替代。重视民族典籍的翻译和研究工作，对于挖掘各民族优秀文化，保护各民族文明，增强各民族之间的沟通和了解，进一步向世界其他地区传播各少数民族优秀文化，乃至提高我国文化软实力都有着重要意义。不少少数民族聚居地处于祖国边疆，有的处在"一带一路"建设关键部位，有的处在与周边国家进行各种交流的重要位置。

中国民族典籍是世界多元文化的有机组成部分，与其他文化共同造就了世界文化的绚丽多姿。世界正因为其文化多样性才变得缤纷多彩。我国各民族典籍中包含的文化多样性极大地丰富了世界多元、特色鲜明的文化。人们对多样性形成全新的认识角度和思维方式。多样性开阔了人们的视野，丰富了人们思考问题的角度。挖掘这些典籍中所蕴含的教育价值和文化价值，对世界其他民族都有指导和借鉴意义，并且有助于建设我国的文化自信。

民族典籍本身蕴含的特殊价值对加强民族文化了解、促进中外文化交流具有重大意义。民族典籍英译具有文学翻译和文化传递之功能，有对外宣传作用，还是一种文学外交。因此，民族典籍翻译和研究对于维护祖国统一、促进民族团结、稳定边疆以及增强国内各民族和中外文化之间的交流都起着极为重要的作用。

中华人民共和国成立以后，中央政府一直十分重视民族典籍翻译和研究工作，提供了强有力的政策支持，并采取了一系列有效措施，加快了各少数民族典籍的抢救、整理、翻译和研究的进程。中央政府多次召开西藏工作会议和新疆工作会议。近年来，国际和国内对于多元文化高度关注，少数民族文学典籍的翻译已然成为业内研究的热点。

近年来，民族典籍翻译和研究迅猛发展，势头良好。国家大力支持，发放国家社科基金课题，教育部和国家民委也发放课题，扶持了一大批研究者。很多民族典籍翻译课题得以立项并顺利开展；为数不少的民族典籍被翻译成汉语、英语和其他语言并出版发行；越来越多的业界人士致力于这个满富生机的学术领域。

在中国文化走出去的国家战略下，全国少数民族典籍英译学术研讨会陆续召开，已经召开三次。

序 一

　　云南是中国民族最多的省份。人口在5000人以上的少数民族有25个,其中有15个民族为云南所特有,分别是:白族、哈尼族、傣族、傈僳族、佤族、拉祜族、纳西族、景颇族、布朗族、普米族、阿昌族、基诺族、怒族、德昂族、独龙族。其中除白族人口占全国白族人口总数的84%以上外,其他14个民族95%居住在云南。

　　云南还是我国跨境民族最多的省份。在云南的25个少数民族中,有16个民族跨境而居,分别是:傣族、壮族、苗族、景颇族、瑶族、哈尼族、德昂族、佤族、拉祜族、彝族、阿昌族、傈僳族、布依族、怒族、布朗族、独龙族。

　　云南少数民族创造了辉煌的文化。据不完全统计,云南少数民族文字文献古籍蕴藏量达10万余册(卷),口传古籍4万余种。云南省民委少数民族古籍整理出版规划办公室为了挽救和保护这些古籍,计划在5年内编纂出版100卷《云南少数民族古籍珍本集成》。这是一个令人瞩目的庞大计划。将这些古籍中的珍品翻译介绍给世界,不仅能够弘扬云南省丰富多彩的民族文化,而且有助于增进与南亚东南亚国家的理解与交流,为"一带一路"倡议的实施做出贡献。

　　云南师范大学外国语学院很重视这一领域的工作。在外国语学院领导支持下,李昌银教授带领一个由教授和中青年学者组成的团队对精选出来的17部云南少数民族经典作品进行英译,计划在5年内("十三五"期间)翻译出版。这是一项十分有意义的宏大工程。

　　这17部民族典籍,内容全部为各民族的英雄史诗或神话传说,具有很高的历史意义和文学价值。这些作品涉及阿昌族、白族、傣族、德昂族、哈尼族、景颇族、拉祜族、苗族、纳西族、普米族、彝族等11个少数民族。

云南师范大学这支翻译队伍实力强大，主要由一些多年从事翻译教学、研究和实践的教授和副教授组成，他们是李昌银、黄瑛、彭庆华、孙兴文、吴相如、刘德周、杨慧芳、郜菊、陈萍、包琼（Joan Cecile Boulerice）等国内外专家学者。他们在云南翻译界都是风云人物。

在民族典籍英译中，这支队伍异军突起，为我国民族典籍英译壮大了声势，必将为中国民族典籍走向世界而成为世界文学的一部分做出新贡献。

民族典籍翻译与研究事业关乎国家的稳定统一，关乎民族关系的和谐发展，关乎世界多元文化的实现。在中国，民族典籍资源极为丰富，有待进一步挖掘、翻译。因此，民族典籍英译前景光明。同时，我们也应意识到，仍有许多濒临消失的少数民族典籍亟待拯救，民族典籍翻译与研究工作任重而道远。

（李正栓，中国英汉语比较研究会典籍英译专业委员会常务副会长兼秘书长、河北师范大学博士生导师）

Foreword by Li Zhengshuan

The translation of Chinese ethnic classics is an important approach in spreading Chinese culture, literature and civilization. It is a crucial component of Chinese culture going global. The spreading of Chinese culture and literature is a national policy and an important way to improve the cultural soft power of China. It plays an indispensable role in the cultural exchange between China and other countries and the development of world literature.

The ethnic groups in China have countless excellent classics with high anthropological, literary and cultural value. The ancestors of each ethnic group have passed down their distinctive culture orally or in writing. Almost all the ethnic groups have their own story of creation, epics, myths and legends.

Chinese ethnic classics are unique and irreplaceable. It is imperative to attach importance to the translation and research of ethnic classics; to explore the excellent ethnic cultures; to protect the civilization of ethnic groups; to enhance the communication and understanding among ethnic groups; to further spread the outstanding culture of ethnic groups to other parts of the world; and to build the cultural strength of China. Many ethnic groups live in the border areas and thus play an important role in the cultural and economic cooperation between China and its neighbors in the context of the Belt and Road Initiative.

Chinese ethnic classics are an important component of the magnificence and diversity of world culture. It is diversity that makes the world so colorful. The cultural diversity of Chinese ethnic classics has greatly enriched the world's pluralism and its distinctive features. People around the world have formed a new understanding of diversity. This diversity has expanded people's horizon and enriched their way of thinking. Digging out the educational and cultural value in these classics can contribute to the construction of China's self-confidence in culture.

The special value of the ethnic classics itself is of great significance to the strengthening of national culture and intercultural communication between China and foreign countries. The translation of ethnic classics is not just a literary exchange, but also a form of cultural communication. It is diplomacy through literature in that it consolidates the cultural ties between China and other countries.

After the founding of the People's Republic of China, the central government attached great importance to the translation and research of ethnic classics, provided a great deal of policy support, and adopted a series of effective measures to speed up the process of rescuing, collating, translating and studying ethnic classics. The central government has convened several working conferences on Tibet and Xinjiang. In recent years, both China and other countries have paid close attention to multiculture. The translation of ethnic classics has become a hot topic.

In recent years, the translation and research of ethnic classics have progressed rapidly and have shown good prospects. The government strongly supports and grants the research projects of the national social science fund. The Ministry of Education and the State Ethnic Affairs Commission are also issuing research projects and giving funding to a large number of researchers. Many research projects on ethnic classics have been approved and carried out. Many ethnic classics have been translated into Chinese, English and other languages and published. More and more professionals have dedicated themselves to this new sphere of learning.

In this context, the academic conferences on translation of ethnic classics are held one after another all around the country. And up to now three have been held.

Yunnan is the province which has the most ethnic groups in China. Besides the Han people, there are 25 ethnic groups, each with a population of more than 5,000. Among them, 15 ethnic groups are unique to Yunnan, which are the Bai, the Hani, the Dai, the Lisu, the Wa, the Lahu, the Naxi, the Jingpo, the Bulang, the Pumi, the Achang, the Jinuo, the Nu, the De'ang and the Dulong. Among these, 84% of the total number of the Bai people in China and 95% of the other 14 ethnic groups are living in Yunnan.

Yunnan is also the province which has the most cross-border ethnic groups. Of the 25 ethnic groups, 16 live across the border, namely: the Dai, the Zhuang, the Miao, the Jingpo, the Yao, the Hani, the De'ang, the Wa, the Lahu, the Yi, the Achang, the Lisu, the Buyi, the Nu, the Bulang and the Dulong.

The ethnic groups in Yunnan have created splendid cultures. According to statistics, the number of classics of Yunnan ethnic groups is more than 100 thousand volumes and classics in oral tradition are more than 40 thousand. In order to save and protect these ancient books, the Office of Classics Collation and Publishing of Yunnan Ethnic Groups Affairs Commission planned to compile and publish 100 volumes of *A Collection of Yunnan Ethnic Group Rare Books* in five years, which is an ambitious plan. The introduction of the ancient classics via translation can not only promote and develop the colorful ethnic cultures of Yunnan, but also contribute to the understanding and exchange between China and countries in South Asia and Southeast Asia and to the implementation of the Belt and Road Initiative as well.

The School of Foreign Languages and Literature of Yunnan Normal University is paying close attention to this field. With the support of the School and the University,

Professor Li Changyin is leading a group of professors and young scholars to do the project of *Classics of Yunnan Ethnic Groups in English Translation*, which includes 17 ethnic classics selected carefully from Yunnan's bountiful ethnic classics. These books are the heroic epics or myths and legends of each ethnic groups with great historical significance and literary value. They will finish the translation in five years (during the Thirteenth Five-Year Plan). After that, all the works will be published by Yunnan People's Publishing House.

The 17 works cover 11 ethnic groups: the Achang, the Bai, the Dai, the De'ang, the Hani, the Jingpo, the Lahu, the Miao, the Naxi, the Pumi and the Yi. All of these groups except the Miao and the Yi are unique to Yunnan.

The translation team of Yunnan Normal University is full of strength and vitality, composed of professors and associate professors who have been occupied in translation teaching, research, and practice for a long time. They are Li Changyin, Huang Ying, Peng Qinghua, Sun Xingwen, Wu Xiangru, Liu Dezhou, Yang Huifang, Gao Ju, Chen Ping, Joan Boulerice and other experts and scholars who are representative figures in the translation field in Yunnan province.

This team is a new force that has suddenly arisen in terms of translating ethnic classics. It is expanding the momentum of ethnic classics translation in China and has made a new contribution for China's ethnic classics to go global and become a part of world literature.

达古达楞格莱标 // Da-gu Da-leng Gelaibiao

The translation and research of ethnic classics are related to the development of Chinese culture and the realization of multiculturalism in the world. In China, ethnic classics are extremely rich in resources, which require us to make further exploration and research and translate them into other languages. Therefore, the future of translating ethnic classics is bright. At the same time, we should also realize that there are still many ethnic works which are close to extinction and urgently need to be rescued. We still have a long way to go in the fields of translation and research in ethnic classics.

(Li Zhengshuan, Standing Vice Chairman and Secretary General, Classics Translation Committee of CACSEC, PhD supervisor at Hebei Normal University)

序 二

◎王 宏

好友云南师范大学外国语学院李昌银教授来电嘱托我为"云南少数民族经典作品英译文库"的出版写一序言,并随即发来该文库的背景资料,让我"不着急,慢慢写"。我本人从事中国典籍英译及研究,深知少数民族典籍对外传译的重要性,但又是少数民族典籍翻译的门外汉。因此,我是怀着虚心学习的态度来写此序言的。近年来,在中国文化"走出去"战略工程大背景下,在中央和地方各级政府的大力支持下,我国少数民族典籍的对外传译及研究工作顺利开展,取得了很大的进步。请看以下数据:

2008年,广西百色学院韩家权教授获批国家社科基金项目《布洛陀史诗》(壮汉英对照)。该项目已顺利结项,并于2013年12月获得中国民间文艺最高奖"山花奖"。

2012年,广西百色学院外语系翻译团队翻译的国家级非物质文化遗产《壮族嘹歌》(英文版)由广西师范大学出版社正式出版。

2012年,东北大学秦皇岛分校吴松林教授主编的《蒙古族系列:江格尔(汉英对照)》(上下册)由吉林大学出版社出版。

2013年,河北师范大学李正栓教授英译《藏族格言诗》

由长春出版社出版发行。

2013年，云南财经大学崔晓霞教授撰写的《〈阿诗玛〉英译研究》收入由王宏印教授主编、民族出版社出版的"民族典籍翻译研究丛书"。

2014年，东北大学秦皇岛分校吴松林教授撰写的《满族档案文献研究》申请到国家社科后期资助，他英译的《英雄格斯尔可汗》由吉林大学出版社出版。

2014年，中南民族大学张立玉教授主持的"土家族主要典籍英译及研究"获批国家社科基金项目。

2015年，西安外国语大学梁真惠副教授撰写的《〈玛纳斯〉翻译传播研究》收入由王宏印教授主编、民族出版社出版的"民族典籍翻译研究丛书"。

与此同时，第一届和第二届全国少数民族典籍英译学术研讨会分别于2012年和2014年在广西民族大学和大连民族学院举行，参加会议的院校分布之广、与会代表数量之众、提交论文数量之多和涉及研究话题之细，十分可喜。2016年还将在中南民族大学举行第三届全国少数民族典籍英译学术研讨会。

为什么少数民族典籍的对外传译及研究工作在短短几年就受到译界的青睐，取得众多成果？我认为，这在很大程度上归于典籍翻译界乃至翻译界同仁对"中国典籍"的重新思考和认识。中国典籍浩如烟海，卷帙浩繁，举世瞩目，是全人类共同的精神财富。但对于中国典籍的理解，我们以前较多限于汉民族的重要文献和书籍，而对少数民族多有忽略。在讨论中国典籍时，也较多关注古代文学作品。其实，中国典籍指"中国清代末年1911年以前的重要文献和书籍",这就要求我们从事典籍翻译时,不但要翻译古代文学典籍作品,还要翻译古代哲学、科技、法律、医学、经济、军事、天文、地理等诸多方面的典籍作品,不但要翻译汉民族的典籍作品,也要翻译各少数民族的典籍作品。

民族典籍具有该民族的原型符号的特质,蕴藏着能够"遗传"并不断"再生"的文化基因。民族典籍是中华传统文化的内核,同时还是中华传统文化的符号构成规则。中国是具有56个民族的多民族国家,少数民族典籍是我国少数民族勤劳与智慧的结晶,是中华文明、也是世界文明不可或缺的一部分。少数民族典籍对外传译具有跨文化交流的作用,它不但有助于更多的人了解少数民族的独特文化,而且还有助于保护少数民族文化的独特性、维持少数民族文化多样性、促进各民族团结、提升中华文化软实力等。

中国少数民族典籍涉及宗教、文学、历史、语言、医学、天文历算等领域,内容丰富,版本多样,载体特殊,传承奇特。仅以《中国少数民族古籍总目提要》为例,该书于1997年正式立项,全书总体设计约60卷、110册,目前已出版23个民族卷共20册:纳西族卷、白族卷、东乡族卷·裕固族卷·保安族卷、土族卷·撒拉族卷、锡伯族卷、哈尼族卷、回族卷·铭刻、柯尔克孜族卷、羌族卷、毛南族卷·京族卷、仫佬族卷、达斡尔族卷、土家族卷、鄂温克族卷、鄂伦春族卷、赫哲族卷、苗族卷、侗族卷、黎族卷、朝鲜族卷。该书真实地反映了我国各少数民族古籍赋存的全面情况,充实了中国的历史和文化内容,为后人探索各种文化形式的源流、揭示中国社会文化发展的轨迹提供了极为珍贵的资料，为我国乃至世界各国人文科学研究提供了一套新颖而全面的资料，对于弘扬中华民族传统文化具有深远的历史意义和现实意义。

少数民族典籍的对外传译是一项艰巨的工作，涉及将少数民族语言译成汉语、少数民族语言之间的互译和少数民族语言译成外语（主要是英语）。前两类翻译历史源远流长，最早可追溯到春秋战国时代《越人歌》的翻译，即汉、壮语之间的翻译。少数民族典籍译成外语的时间则要晚一些。据考证，维吾尔族古典长诗《福乐智慧》成书于1069年或1070年，目前尚未发现完整的原稿，只存留下来三个抄本，分别为赫拉特抄本、费尔干纳抄本与埃及抄本，其中费尔干纳抄本于12~13世纪用阿拉伯文纳斯赫体抄写，1914年发现于今中亚乌孜别克斯坦纳曼干城，现存于该共和国科学院东方研究所。这是少数民族典籍译介到国外的最早纪录。少数民族典籍外译在现代有了较快发展。一些少数民族典籍，如藏族的《格萨尔王传》、蒙古族的《江格尔》和柯尔克孜族的《玛纳斯》等英雄史诗，云南彝族的《阿诗玛》、维吾尔族的《艾里甫和赛乃姆》等民间叙事长诗已先后被翻译成英语及其他外国文字，为世人所知。这对传承少数民族经典，推动中外文化交流起到了不可替代的作用。然而，还有大量的中国少数民族典籍等待我们去翻译和研究。

云南省少数民族典籍资源十分丰富。据不完全统计，云南少数民族文字文献古籍蕴藏量达10万余册（卷），口传古籍4万余种。"云南少数民族经典作品英译文库"正是依托云南省丰富的少数民族典籍资源，借助云南师范大学外国语学院强大的翻译师资队伍，在云南人民出版社的有力支持下，首次将云南少数民族经典作品成系列对外译介的大力举措。云南师范大学外国语学院对"云南少数民族经典作品英译文库"十分重视，他们首先邀请省内外少数民族语言文化研究专家对云南民族典籍和民族文化经典作品进行筛选，做到"好中选好，优中选优"，同时调配最强的翻译力量承担文库的翻译任务。我粗略看了该文库的选题，发现选题面广，覆盖范围宽，收入了云南省阿昌族、白族、傣族、纳西族、德昂族、哈尼族、景颇族、拉祜族、苗族、普米族和彝族等民族的典籍作品。云南共有25个少数民族，其中11个少数民族的典籍作品都覆盖到了，不少作品还是首次译成英文。这将彻底改变云南少数民族典籍由于对外译介数量较少，不为世界了解的尴尬局面。

对于云南师范大学外国语学院而言，把少数民族典籍英译作为翻译专业的优势特色进行建设，这将对该院的学科建设起到助推作用。"云南少数民族经典作品英译文库"所产生的翻译成果和研究成果将培养出一批优秀的典籍翻译和研究团队，凸显该院在全国的学术特色和学术影响，同时还能将翻译能力和研究能力转化为教学能力，提高云南师范大学外国语学院翻译专业研究生的培养质量，为社会输送高水平的翻译人才，有力地支撑学院翻译专业学科的建设和发展。我对云南师范大学外国语学院的翻译师资队伍较为熟悉。作为云南省唯一获得省级高校优势特色学科建设项目的外国语学院，该院具有雄厚的翻译师资力量，在云南省各高校中当属第一。多年来，该院翻译与跨文化研究团队一直承担着对外交流与合作的各种口笔译项目及任务。由外国语学院精心挑选和确定的"云南少数民族经典作品英译文库"翻译人员绝大多数都是云南省翻译领域里的知名教授或专家,有国外留学经历,且具有扎实的英汉双语语言功底,曾翻译出版多部译著和翻译作品,并且主持和参与过多项翻译项目的研究。我阅读李昌银教授发来的文库翻译人员名单,发现多名我所熟悉的知名教授、博士也在其中,感到格外放心。

"云南少数民族经典作品英译文库"的出版发行是云南省翻译界的一件大事,也是我国少数民族典籍翻译传来的又一佳音。想当年,我和"大中华文库"总协调人李林老师曾在参加全国典籍英译学术研讨会之余一起找到李昌银教授,敦促李教授向学校和同事呼吁,少数民族典籍翻译及研究是富矿,值得快挖、深挖,能早出成果,出大成果。今天,我们当年的心愿变成了美好的现实,心里感到特别高兴。再次热烈祝贺"云南少数民族经典作品英译文库"的顺利出版!

(王宏,中国典籍翻译研究会副会长、苏州大学博士生导师)

Foreword by Wang Hong

My friend Professor Li Changyin of Yunnan Normal University asked me to write a few words for the publication of *Classics of Yunnan Ethnic Groups in English Translation*. I am more than delighted to do it. As I have been doing research in English translation of Chinese classics, I know how important this work is. In recent years, substantial progress has been made in translating Chinese ethnic classics into English and introducing them to the world. Let's look at the following accomplishments.

First of all, several projects in the English translation of ethnic classics have received funding from the National Planning Office of Philosophy and Social Science. The first of these projects is *The Epic of Baeuqloxgdoh* (Zhuang-Chinese-English trilingual version), given funding in 2008 and headed by Professor Han Jiaquan of Baise University in Guangxi Zhuang Autonomous Region. In December 2013, this translation won the Shanhua Award, the most prestigious prize for folk literature and art in China. The second project is *A Study of the Manchu Archives*, written by Professor Wu Songlin of Northeastern University at Qinhuangdao and which was given funding in 2014. The third is *English*

Translation and Study of the Major Classics of the Tujia Ethnic Group, headed by Professor Zhang Liyu of the South-Central University for Nationalities, also granted in 2014.

Secondly, several English translations have been published. In 2012, *Liao Songs of Pingguo Zhuang*, has been listed as one of China's national intangible cultural heritages. It was translated by the School of Foreign Languages, Baise University, and published by Guangxi Normal University Press. Also in 2012, *Jangar* (a Chinese-English bilingual edition), edited by Professor Wu Songlin of Northeastern University at Qinhuangdao, was published by Jilin University Press. In 2013, *Tibetan Gnomic Verses Translated into English*, translated by Professor Li Zhengshuan of Hebei Normal University, was published by Changchun Press. And in 2014, *Heroic Geser Khan*, translated by Professor Wu Songlin of Northeastern University at Qinhuangdao, was published by Jilin University Press.

And thirdly, two important monographs have been published by The Ethnic Publishing House in the *Ethnic Classics Translation Research Series* edited by Professor Wang Hongyin of Nankai University. One is *A Study on the English Translation of* Ashima *by Gladys Taylor* (2013), which was the PhD dissertation of Professor Cui Xiaoxia of Yunnan University of Finance and Economics. The other is *Translation and Dissemination of the Oral Epic Manas* (2015) written by Associate Professor Liang Zhenhui of Xi'an International

Studies University.

Meanwhile, it is encouraging to see that the first conferences on English translation of ethnic classics in China have been held in Guangxi Nationalities University and Dalian Nationalities Institute respectively. Participants were both many and enthusiastic. Many papers were presented and a lot of topics discussed. The third conference will be hosted by South Central Nationalities University in 2016.

Why, then, has this field attracted so much attention from translators and scholars alike and accomplished so much in just a few years? The answer, I believe, lies in a rethinking of what constitutes Chinese classics as an indispensable part of human heritage. We used to see Chinese classics as more or less equal to the classics of the Han people, excluding works by other ethnic groups. Moreover, when we talk about Chinese classics, we focus too much on the literary works of ancient times. Yet Chinese classics actually refer to "important works and books before 1911, the year when the Qing dynasty fell, bringing an end to imperial rule". This definition requires us to pay attention not just to literary works, but also writings in other subjects, such as philosophy, science, law, medicine, economics, military affairs, astronomy, and geography, not only Han works, but writings by other ethnic groups as well.

The classical works of a nation are its archetypal symbols, the major carriers of its cultural genes. Chinese classics make up the core of Chinese tradition. The Chinese nation consists of 56 ethnic groups. Ethnic classics are an important part of not only Chinese traditional culture, but also world civilization. The translation of these works into other languages is important in that it helps to promote cross-cultural communications between China and other countries and to protect and preserve the uniqueness and diversity of ethnic cultures by making them accessible to foreign readers.

Chinese ethnic classics cover a variety of areas, such as religion, literature, history, language, medicine, astrology, and calendar, with numerous editions, special media and unique ways of transmission from generation to generation. Take, for example, *An Anthology of Chinese Ethnic Classics*, a colossal project that includes 110 volumes, 20 of which, from 23 ethnic groups, have been published. The anthology reflects the variety and quantity of China's ethnic classics and provides valuable material and resources for studying, understanding and developing Chinese culture and history in a more comprehensive and sustainable way.

The translation of Chinese ethnic classics into foreign languages is a very demanding job, involving rendering from ethnic languages to Chinese, between ethnic languages, and from ethnic languages (often via Chinese) to foreign languages. The first two types of translation can be traced back to the Spring and Autumn Period, when *The Song of the Yue People* was translated from their mother tongue into Chinese. The earliest translation of ethnic classics into a foreign language is *Wisdom of Royal Glory*, a long poem of the Uygurs, which was rendered from the source language into Arabic and is now in the Oriental Institute of Uzbekistan at Namangan. But it was not until modern times that the translation of ethnic classics into foreign languages accelerated. Noticeably, ethnic epics, such as *The Story of Prince Geser* of the Tibetans, *The Story of Jianggeer* of the Mongolians, *Manas* of the Kyrgyz, and narrative poems such as *Ashima* of the Yi people, *Alip and Salam* of the Uygurs, etc., have been published. These translations have contributed to acquainting the world with Chinese ethnic classics, but many remain to be translated.

Yunnan is rich in ethnic classics, boasting more than 100,000 volumes of written classics and over 40,000 pieces of oral literature. Relying on such bountiful resources, as a collective endeavor of the translation team of the School of Foreign Languages and Literature, Yunnan Normal University and with the help of Yunnan People's Publishing House, *Classics of Yunnan Ethnic Groups in English Translation* is the first project to translate Yunnan ethnic classics into English on a large scale. The School adheres to a professional spirit and academic standard in carrying out the project by selecting the most authoritative texts in the source language (Chinese) and recruiting the best translators from its huge faculty. The selection of the works, covering eleven of the twenty-five ethnic groups of the province, indicates expertise and insight. The implementation of the project will change the embarrassing obscurity of Yunnan ethnic classics by making them known to the world, many of them for the first time.

In light of disciplinary development, the project is of great importance, too. Participating in the translation will strengthen the academic foundation of the teachers, enrich their experience and enhance their translation skills and research ability. This in turn will help them become better teachers and thus able to educate students with higher quality. The publication of the books will add greatly to the faculty accomplishments of the School and raise the academic standing of Yunnan Normal University by taking the first step in this direction among the universities of Yunnan province.

This publication project is a great event not only for Yunnan itself, but also for China. Looking back, I remember that Professor Li Changyin, our friend Li Lin, editor of the *Library of Chinese Classics*, and I talked enthusiastically about initiating something like this in Yunnan when we attended a conference on the translation of ethnic classics in Soochow. Lin and I strongly suggested that Professor Li do it as soon as possible. Now I am very pleased to see our talk becoming reality. Again, my congratulations on the publication of *Classics of Yunnan Ethnic Groups in English Translation*!

(Wang Hong, Vice Chairman of Classics Translation Committee of CACSEC, PhD supervisor at Soochow University)

导　言

"云南少数民族经典作品英译文库"旨在将云南少数民族的经典作品翻译介绍给国外对其感兴趣的英文读者大众。随着以古代汉文经典构成的"大中华文库"的出版发行，学界正将注意力转移到民族典籍的翻译上来。民族典籍是指由民族作家创作的反应民族历史和文化的经典作品。广西、贵州、辽宁、新疆、西藏等省区的大学已经捷足先登。我们云南也理应有所作为。云南拥有全国最多的少数民族。全省25个少数民族中，有15个为云南特有民族，即阿昌族、白族、布朗族、傣族、德昂族、独龙族、哈尼族、景颇族、基诺族、拉祜族、傈僳族、纳西族、怒族、普米族、佤族。这些民族的典籍，有的是原作，有的是汉译本，构成了一个巨大的宝库，我们有义务将其介绍给国外的英语读者和学术界。问题是，先译什么？

云南所有的25个少数民族都创造了自己的经典作品，包括史诗、神话、创世故事、民谣、戏曲、山歌和丧歌，以各种形式流传于各地，总数不下10万卷，这还不包括口传文体。经过调查研究，并征求民族学专家的建议后，我们决定重点翻译史诗和神话。史诗和神话叙述的是民族起源故事，最能反映各民族哲学、历史、文化等的概貌、渊源。我们从汗牛充栋的民族史诗与神话中精选了云南阿昌族、白族、傣族、德昂族、哈尼族、景颇族、拉祜族、苗族、纳西族、普米族、彝族等 11 个少数民族的 17 部最具有代表性的经典作品。这些作品全部都是汉语译本，由既会讲母语又精通汉语的双语学者整理、翻译而成。其中有的是在节庆仪式和表演时从口语录制而来。我们没有选择用民族语言写成的文本，首先是因为很难寻找到民族语和英语俱佳的译者；其次是因为一部分典籍的民族语言文本在民间以多种方言形式流传，情节五花八门。汉语文本系专家仔细整理、翻译而成，因而更具权威性。接下来的问题是：如何译？

在我们选定的 17 部作品中，除了《白国因由》为散文体之外，其余全部为民歌韵文体，诗行长度大致相当，行末有松散押韵，无格律。译诗为诗是最起码的要求。我们遵循的原则有如下几点。

一、若原文为诗歌，译文也必须为诗歌。

二、译文尽可能完整地再现原文的思想内容和意象。

三、译文尽可能再现原文的修辞手段。

四、不改变原文每一节诗的行数，除非万不得已。

五、不使用英文的标准格律，因为原文并不是标准的格律体。采用英文的自然节奏，但诗行长短应大体一致。

六、不用韵，除非符合英文表达习惯且不损害原文内容。

我们所追求的，用苏珊·巴斯奈特的话来说就是"异地播种"，而不是直接移栽树木。关于原文的形式特征，尤其是尾韵，能再现时再现，不能再现时果断放弃。

那谁来翻译呢？本文库是云南师范大学外国语学院的集体项目，因此我们的翻译团队由本院十几位同行加上两位在职攻读翻译专业硕士学位的高校教师组成。所有译者都在高校教授翻译课程，从事翻译研究，不仅发表了翻译论文，也出版了译著。

  传统上，人们通常是将外语译为母语，而不是将母语译为外语。但是这种情况正在发生改变。现在许多译者都将母语译为外语。根据耐克·帕科恩[①]和斯图亚特·坎贝尔[②]的论证，将母语译入非母语，能够达到相当高的水平。中国的情形为他们的观点提供了新的论据。中国典籍英译在19世纪由英国汉学家理雅各和翟理斯发起，20世纪在亚瑟·伟利、戴维·霍克思、波顿·沃森、约翰·闵福德、宇文所安等英美汉学家的推动下继续发展。值得注意的是，在这一过程中，旅居西方的华人学者迅速加入到了中国典籍英译的行列中。其中最著名的是辜鸿铭和林语堂。他们主动承担这个任务，因为他们认为西方汉学家的母语并非汉语，其译文往往误读汉语原文本，误解中国文化，自己义不容辞，必须为英语读者提供更忠实的英文翻译。自20世纪50年代开始，越来越多的中国大陆译者投身于典籍英译或重译。在杨宪益、许渊冲、汪榕培、王宏印、王宏、李正栓等当代翻译家和翻译理论家的积极倡导和引领下，典籍英译蔚然成风，势头强劲。许渊冲、王宏、李正栓等都在西方出版社出版了英文译著，这表明他们的英文水平达到了国际上的出版标准。

  就本文库而言，我们采取了一系列保障译文质量的措施。我们要求译者尽最大努力拿出代表自己最高水平的译文。文

---

① 挑战公理：译入非母语.阿姆斯特丹：约翰·本杰明斯出版公司，2005.
② 译入第二语言.纽约：劳特里奇出版社，2013.

库的主编们对译文进行仔细研读，纠正理解偏差、语法错误以及格式上的问题。在此基础上，我们采取了一个不可或缺的步骤，请长期在我院从事英语教学工作的美国老师包琼（Joan Cecile Boulerice）对每一个译本进行逐字逐句的修改，使之更自然流畅，更符合英文表达习惯。我们尽了最大的努力。如果译文还存在什么问题，皆由我们负责，与包琼老师无关。

　　在这里，我们对所有给予我们宝贵帮助和支持的专家学者深表谢忱。感谢云南人民出版社的领导为文库成功申报为"十三五"国家重点出版物出版规划项目和国家出版基金项目给予的大力支持。感谢文库责编、东南亚南亚读物编辑部主任郭木玉，她的严谨和敬业令我们动容。感谢云南师范大学为文库提供了出版资金支持，使译者们不被"眼前的苟且"干扰，能够一心一意地追求"诗和远方"。感谢李正栓教授和王宏教授不仅一直鼓励我们前进，而且欣然为文库作序，从全球视野对其意义进行肯定，极大地提振了我们的信心。感谢包琼老师，她的修改保证了译文的流畅性。最后要特别感谢王宏教授和湖南人民出版社的资深编辑李林先生，是他们的建议促成了本文库的构想。

云南师范大学外国语学院
"云南少数民族经典作品英译文库"编委会

General Introduction

This publication project, *Classics of Yunnan Ethnic Groups in English Translation*, aims at introducing Yunnan ethnic classical works to the world by making them available to native speakers of English who might be interested in them. With the publication of the *Library of Chinese Classics*, which consists only of books written by Han authors in classical Chinese, attention now is being turned to the English translation and publication of ethnic classics, books produced by ethnic writers about their history and culture. Universities in provinces such as Guangxi, Guizhou, Liaoning, Xinjiang, and Xizang, have taken the initiative. We in Yunnan must do something, because Yunnan has the largest number of ethnic groups in China. 15 of the 25 ethnic groups in the province, the Achang, the Bai, the Bulang, the Dai, the De'ang, the Dulong, the Hani, the Jingpo, the Jinuo, the Lahu, the Lisu, the Naxi, the Nu, the Pumi, and the Wa, live in no other place but Yunnan. The classics of these people, either in their own language or in Chinese translations, are a great treasure house, which should be accessible to English readers and scholars. But what works should be translated first?

All the 25 ethnic groups in Yunnan have their classics,

epics, mythology, creation stories, folksongs, folk drama, mountain songs, and funeral lament lyrics, most of which exist in different versions in different places. According to one estimation, there are more than 100,000 volumes of them, excluding those in oral form. After a thorough survey and extensive consultations with experts of ethnic studies, we concluded that priority must be given to epics and mythologies, as they reflect an ethnic people's philosophy, history and culture more than anything else by narrating the stories of where and how they think they came from. From many epics and mythologies, we selected 17 of the most authoritative and popular classics representing 11 Yunnan ethnic groups, the Achang, the Bai, the Dai, the De'ang, the Hani, the Jingpo, the Lahu, the Miao, the Naxi, the Pumi, and the Yi. These works are all in Chinese, translated from the original by bilingual scholars whose mother tongue is their own ethnic language and who are fluent and proficient in Chinese. Some were recorded from their oral form at rituals and performances. We did not choose texts written in the ethnic language, not least because it is very hard to find a translator who is skilled in both the ethnic language and English. Moreover, some of the classics in the ethnic language were circulated in various oral forms and fragments. The published Chinese versions have been carefully edited and translated, hence they are more reliable. The next question is: how to translate them?

It happens that all of the 17 works except one are in verse form, with lines more or less the same length and loose rhymes, but no regular meter. A poem must be rendered into a poem; anything less is unacceptable. So here are the general rules we follow when doing the translation.

One. If the original is verse, the translated text must be verse, too.

Two. Reproduce the ideas and the images of the original as completely as possible.

Three. Reproduce the figures of speech of the original as much as possible.

Four. Do not change the number of lines in a stanza unless absolutely necessary.

Five. Do not use standard meters in English, because the Chinese original does not follow any regular meter. Use the natural rhythm of English instead, but most of the lines should look more or less the same length.

Six. Do not use rhyme unless it comes naturally and is faithful to the content of the original.

What we try to do is, to use Susan Bassnett's words, "transplant the seed", not the tree itself. As for the various aspects of form, particularly meter and end rhyme, we reproduce them when it is possible and abandon them when it is necessary.

Who will do the translations? As this is a collective project of the School of Foreign Languages and Literature of Yunnan Normal University, our team consists of a dozen faculty members and two students from our MA translation program who are already teachers in other universities. All the translators have been teaching translation and doing translation research for a long time. They have published not just academic articles on translation, but also translated books from English to Chinese or vice versa.

Traditionally, people translate into their mother tongue, not into a foreign language. But the situation is changing. Many translators today are translating from their mother tongue into a foreign language. The quality can be good, as Nike K. Pokorn and Stuart Campbell prove in *Challenging the Traditional Axioms: Translation into a non-mother tongue* (Amsterdam: John Benjamins Publishing Company, 2005) and *Translation into the Second Language* (New York: Routledge, 2013) respectively. The case of China provides further evidence for their argument. The translation of Chinese classics into English was initiated by James Legge and Herbert Allen Giles in the 19th century and carried on in the 20th century by Arthur Waley, David Hawkes, Burton Watson, John Minford, Stephen Owen and others. It is noticeable that these English and American sinologists were soon joined by Chinese scholars residing in the West, such as Hongming (Tomson) Gu and Lin Yutang, among others. They took up the job because they thought it was their obligation to give English readers more faithful translations than Western sinologists could, who, as their target language is their mother tongue, often misinterpret the original text and misrepresent Chinese culture. Since the 1950s, there has been an increasingly powerful trend for Mainland Chinese translators to render or re-render Chinese classics into foreign languages, English in particular. In our time, this work is gathering momentum, enthusiastically advocated and actively practiced by such well-known translation experts as Yang Xianyi of Beijing Foreign Language Press, Xu Yuanchong of Beijing University, Wang Rongpei of Dalian Foreign Language Institute, Wang Hongyin of Nankai University, Wang Hong of Soochow University, Li Zhengshuan of Hebei Normal University, and many more. These professors are not just translators, but also scholars in translation studies. More importantly, some of them, Xu Yuanchong, Wang Hong and Li Zhengshuan, for example, have had their translations published by Western publishers, which suggests that their English meets the international standard.

In the case of our project, we request that the translators do their best to produce good translations. When they submit them to us, they should represent the highest level that they can attain. Then the general editors appointed by the School read the translated texts and remove inaccurate renderings and grammar mistakes if there are any. On top of that, we've taken an indispensable measure to ensure that our English is readable. We asked Ms. Joan Cecile Boulerice, an American teacher who has been teaching English in our school since 2009, to read every text that we've translated and improve the English by making it more natural and idiomatic. This is the best we can do. Of course any problems that still remain in the translations are ours. They have nothing to do with our American teacher.

As the project is well under way, we would like to thank all those who have helped to make it possible. Ms. Guo Muyu, director of the South and Southeast Asia Editorial Department, Yunnan People's Publishing House, has been most helpful in our cooperation. In addition, she has added importance to the project by turning it into a national publication project. Yunnan Normal University has supported us by paying the publication fees so that the translators won't have to be burdened with the financial responsibilities for this project. Professor Li Zhengshuan and Professor Wang Hong not only have always encouraged us to go on but have also written the forewords for the project, putting it in a global perspective. Ms. Joan Cecile Boulerice's revision has ensured the fluency of the translated texts. Finally, special thanks must be given to Professor Wang Hong, again, and Mr. Li Lin of Hunan People's Press for their suggestion that has helped us conceive the project from the very beginning.

The General Editors
School of Foreign Languages & Literature
Yunnan Normal University, Kunming

达古达楞格莱标

目 录

序　歌 // 1

天和地的由来 // 5

葫芦人的传说 // 11

茶树、粮种和衣饰的来历 // 79

太阳王子和龙公主 // 129

王宫斩龙 // 155

漫漫坎坷迁徙路 // 173

译后记 // 244

Da-gu Da-leng Gelaibiao

Contents

Prologue // 1

The Origin of the Sky and the Earth // 5

The Legend of the Gourd People // 11

The Origin of Tea Trees, Grain Seeds and Clothes // 79

The Sun Prince and the Dragon Princess // 129

Killing the Dragon in the Royal Palace // 155

A Long and Arduous Journey of Migration // 173

Translator's Afterword // 246

序歌
Prologue

达古达楞格莱标 // Da-gu Da-leng Gelaibiao

父老乡亲聚一堂,
听我来把古歌唱。
世界起源达古传,
人类来历达楞讲。
吃饭莫忘耕田苦,
饮水别忘寻水难。
古歌同山一起生,
德昂历史江河长。
老人一生吃的盐,
比那儿孙吃饭多。
老人一生过的桥,
比起儿孙走路长。
老人唱歌就爱在,
德昂人家火塘旁。
古歌就是德昂本,
世世代代内心藏。
父老乡亲听仔细,
要将古歌永传扬。

序歌
Prologue

Kinfolks, come and sit.

I'll sing for you an old song.

Da-gu talks about the origin of the world,

And Da-leng talks about the origin of humans.

While eating rice, bear in mind the hardship of plowing the field.

While drinking water, bear in mind the hardship of searching for water.

The old song was born with the mountains,

And the history of the De'ang people is as long as the rivers.

The salt an old man has eaten all his life

Is more than the rice his children and grandchildren have had.

The bridges an old man has crossed

Are longer than the road his children and grandchildren have walked.

When an old man sings songs,

He loves to sit by the fire pit.

The old song is the history of the De'ang people,

Which generations to come should carry in their hearts.

Kinfolks, please listen carefully

And sing it to your children when you are old.

天和地的由来

The Origin of the Sky and the Earth

过去无量久远时，
世界混沌分不清。
那时没有天与地，
没有日月与辰星。
此时出现二尊神，
相约来把混沌分。
一神化作公公貌，
公公首先把天造。
一神化作婆婆貌，
婆婆接着把地造。
因为女人贪心多，
大地造得比天阔。
公公一看把眉皱，
把天盖地盖不周。
于是左手擎天空，
右手将地拉扯拢。
从此大地被天覆，
从此大地多起伏。
高处变成岭与山，
低处变成沟谷川。

天和地的由来
The Origin of the Sky and the Earth

Once upon a time,

The world was in a state of chaos.

There was no sky or earth,

Nor was there sun, moon, or stars.

Then there appeared two deities,

Who decided to bring order to the chaos.

One changed into an old man,

Whose first work was to create the sky.

The other turned into an old woman,

Whose first work was to create the earth.

Women were usually greedier than men,

So the earth was wider than the sky.

The old man saw it and frowned:

The sky was not wide enough to cover the earth.

Holding the sky with his left hand,

He shrank the earth with his right hand.

From then on the earth has been covered by the sky;

Since then the earth has bumps and pits.

High places became hills and mountains,

And low places became plains and valleys.

今日青天此来由，

今日大地如是有。

天和地的由来
The Origin of the Sky and the Earth

This is how the blue sky came into being,

And this is how the earth came into being.

葫芦人的传说
The Legend of the Gourd People

一

过去无量久远时，

人类品行渐渐失。

争权夺利人横蛮，

恃强凌弱恶尽沾。

不孝父母只为己，

老弱妇孺遭苦难。

男女不结夫妻缘，

恩义家庭个个散。

骄奢淫逸声色害，

好比禽兽人伦丧。

人间此景即将招，

三灾[①]灭顶无生还。

观见此情混西迦[②]，

[①] 三灾：据佛经载，三灾有小三灾和大三灾之分。此处所说的三灾更接近于佛典所说之大三灾，即当此世界坏灭之时所发生的火灾、水灾与风灾。但与佛典所载不同的是，佛典中三灾发生时，天界也遭到毁坏，而《达古达楞格莱标》中三灾发生时，天界并没有受到影响。

[②] 混西迦：佛典中汉语音译为"释提桓因"，意为"天帝释"，三十三天（帝释天）的天主，亦即我国民间传说的玉皇大帝，主宰人间祸福。德昂族和傣族称为"混西迦"。

葫芦人的传说
The Legend of the Gourd People

I

Once upon a time,

Human manners and behavior were gradually eroding.

People became cruel and fought for power and property.

They bullied the weak and did all kinds of bad deeds.

They were selfish and were not kind to their parents,

And treated women and children especially badly.

Husband and wife did not love each other,

And all affectionate families broke up.

They were destroyed by a luxurious and decadent life,

As they behaved like beasts and forgot about human morality.

Such bad behavior would soon cause Three Catastrophes[①],

Which would spare no human life on the earth.

Hun Xijia[②], the Emperor of Heaven, saw this,

---

① Three Catastrophes: According to Buddhist sutras, Three Catastrophes refers to Three Major Catastrophes and Three Minor Catastropes. In this context, Three Catastrophes refers to three major catastrophes that happened when the universe was destroyed, i.e. fire catastrophe, flood catastrophe and wind catastrophe. One difference from what is recorded in Buddhist sutras is that the De'ang people's folk song *Da-gu Da-leng Gelaibiao* says the Heavenly World was intact.

② Hun Xijia: According to Buddhist sutras, Hun Xijia is the name used by both the De'ang and the Dai ethnic groups to refer to the ruler of the thirty three layers of heaven, i.e. the Jade Emperor of Chinese literature, who controls the human world and decides on the misfortunes and happiness of the human world.

为留人种急下凡。

四处来把人种选,

无奈人无半个贤。

只好找来八神仙,

作为人种留人间。

天帝①拿出宝葫芦,

将八神仙藏里面。

葫芦下面最宽敞,

八仙暂居在此间。

葫芦上面狭又窄,

内藏动物种类鲜。

最后又在葫芦口,

百层莲花作庄严。

莲花光色极妙好,

金色袈裟藏其间。

以此预示三灾后,

帕惹②人间来示现。

琅叨干帕③即此是,

---

① 天帝:混西迦。
② 帕惹:德昂族和傣族对佛祖的称谓。
③ 琅叨干帕:傣文佛典用语(德昂族无文字,传统使用傣文),"琅叨"即葫芦,"干帕"为劫,琅叨干帕就是葫芦劫的意思。

葫芦人的传说
The Legend of the Gourd People

And hurried down to the earth to preserve some human seeds.

He went around and tried to select good human seeds,

But no one was virtuous.

He had to find eight immortals,

And left them on the earth to become human seeds.

The Emperor of Heaven[①] took out a gourd,

In which he hid the eight immortals.

The bottom of the gourd was the most spacious part,

And there the eight immortals stayed.

The upper part of the gourd was long and narrow,

Where a few species of animals were hidden.

And then at the mouth of the gourd

Was decorated with a lotus of a hundred layers.

The lotus gave out a wonderful light,

And in it a golden Kasāya was hidden.

All this was a sign that following the three catastrophes

Pare[②] would be born into the world.

This is called Langdao Ganpa[③],

---

① The Emperor of Heaven: Hun Xijia.
② Pare: It is the name given to Buddha by the De'ang people and the Dai people.
③ Langdao Ganpa: a term in the Dai Buddhist scripture, meaning Catastrophe of the Gourd. The De'ang people do not have written language, so they traditionally use the Dai language. "Langdao" means gourd, "Ganpa" means catastrophe.

达古达楞格莱标 // Da-gu Da-leng Gelaibiao

莫弄干帕① 名又兼。

劫火不久即来袭,

熊熊大火烧天地。

世间万物遭浩劫,

生灵个个灰烟灭。

天地劫火熄未寒,

大地处处似木炭。

接着天地巨风狂,

烧焦万物尘灰茫。

巨风过后洪水来,

大地又变海汪洋。

洪水退去无一存,

唯有葫芦放光芒。

八位神仙藏于中,

三灾过后竟无恙。

此时异香漫天下,

其味似烤糯米粑②。

如此香味自土出,

如此香土遍八方。

---

① 莫弄干帕:傣文佛典用语,"莫弄"即大莲花,"干帕"为劫,莫弄干帕就是大莲花劫的意思。
② 糯米粑:德昂族传统食物,用糯米饭舂制,一般在农历新年前制作。

The Legend of the Gourd People

Or Monong Ganpa[①].

The fire catastrophe came quite soon,

And a huge fire burst out between the sky and the earth.

All things in the world were destroyed,

And all the creatures turned to ash.

No sooner had the fire cooled down

Than the earth became like burnt charcoal.

Then a gale started to blow

And carried the ash everywhere.

A flood struck after the gale,

And the earth turned into a vast sea.

When the flood receded,

Only the gourd survived and shone.

The eight immortals hidden in the gourd

Were safe and sound after the three catastrophes.

Just then a special aroma spread all over,

And it smelled like toasted glutinous rice cakes[②].

The smell came from the soil,

And everywhere was full of the aroma.

---

① Monong Ganpa: a term in the Dai Buddhist scripture, meaning Catastrophe of Lotus. "Monong" means lotus, "Ganpa" means catastrophe.
② Glutinous rice cakes: the De'ang people's traditional food, usually made before the lunar new year.

香味飘进葫芦里,

八位神仙被熏馋。

于是皆从葫芦出,

个个争把香土餐。

大家越吃越想吃,

吃得体圆步蹒跚。

岂料再也飞不动,

神仙国度不能还。

只好打消回去想,

个个垂头把气丧。

此时巨型葫芦里,

动物欲出叫嚷嚷。

于是天帝派雷神,

下凡要将动物放。

雷神先自百层莲,

取出金色袈裟宝。

混尚弄①处来珍藏,

待帕惹出作供养。

然后雷神举神斧,

想要劈开葫芦关。

正欲劈时忽听见,

---

① 混尚弄:"大天神"之意。德昂族和傣族共同的称谓。

葫芦人的传说
The Legend of the Gourd People

The smell floated into the gourd,

And the eight immortals smelled it and became hungry.

So they all came out of the gourd

And greedily ate the fragrant soil.

The more they ate, the more they wanted,

And eventually they became fat and moved with difficulty.

Because they were too fat to fly,

They could not return to their fairyland.

They had to abandon the idea of returning home,

And each bent his head in despair.

At the same time in the giant gourd,

The animals wanted to come out and cried loudly.

The Emperor of Heaven sent the thunder god,

Whose task was to release the animals.

From the lotus of a hundred layers,

The thunder god took out the golden Kasāya first.

He hid it at Hun Shangnong[①]'s place,

Ready to offer it to Pare once he was born.

The thunder god raised his powerful axe

To cut open the mouth of the gourd.

He was just about to split open the gourd

---

① Hun Shangnong: It means "great heaven deity". The De'ang people and the Dai people share the same term for the same meaning.

各种动物齐叫喊:
"左边有我不能劈!
右边有我不能砍!"
……
上下左右都试过,
都有动物来叫喊。
雷神无奈把心狠,
一斧劈开葫芦口。
螃蟹倒霉头被砍,
从此螃蟹没了头。
于是葫芦诸动物,
个个得从葫芦出。

那时世间无女人,
八位神仙都是男。
彼时大家在一起,
快乐无忧同生息。
饿了就以香土食,
饱足仍复共嬉戏。
那时人兽和睦处,
那时动物种类稀。
于是八仙用香土,

The Legend of the Gourd People

When he heard the animals inside shouting,

"I am on the left side, don't cut this side!"

"I am on the right side, don't cut this side!"

…

Every time he tried to cut a side of the gourd,

He heard some animals crying from that side.

The thunder god had no choice but to be cruel;

He swung the axe and cleaved the opening of the gourd.

The crab was unlucky and had his head cut off,

And ever since then crabs have no heads.

Now all the animals in the gourd

Came out of the gourd.

There were no women at that time,

And the eight immortals were all men.

They lived together,

And felt happy without any worries.

They ate the fragrant soil when they were feeling hungry,

And played for fun when they were full.

There was peace between the men and the animals,

Of which there were only a few species.

So the eight immortals made use of the fragrant soil,

捏成各类动物躯。
飞禽抛空即会飞，
走兽落地就奔驱。
彼分雄雌八仙见，
相互交配后代衍。
于是辗转念念想，
没有女人怎繁衍？
为此大家齐聚首，
共把今后来商研。
八仙最后齐决定，
选出四仙变女人。
结果谁人也不愿，
甘心情愿做女眷。
只好共同盟誓约，
分开来把大地圈。
四仙向着东方走，
向西前行另四仙。
相遇谁方先开口，
谁方就将女身变。
于是双方齐动身，
日夜兼程不休闲。
不知行了多少月，

葫芦人的传说
The Legend of the Gourd People

And molded it into various animal shapes.

Birds could fly once they were thrown into the air,

And animals could run once they were put on the ground.

The eight immortals found that the animals were divided

Into male and female, who thus mated and multiplied.

Then they hit upon an idea:

How could they reproduce without women?

And for that reason they all came together

And had a discussion about their future.

The eight immortals finally decided

That they would choose four of them to become women.

But none of them

Was willing to be a woman.

They had to come to an agreement:

They would walk around the earth.

Four of them would go eastward,

And the other four westward.

When they met again,

The group speaking first would be changed into females.

They then set off at the same time,

And traveled day and night without rest.

They were not sure how many months or years

不知走过多少年。
由于分开太长久，
早将誓约忘天边。
最后双方忽相遇，
向西四仙先开言。
于是四仙变女人，
男人仍为东行仙。
从此八人结双对，
从此人间情欲添。
从此始有四家庭，
从此人类始生衍。

那时不知时暂久，
岁月如流任悠悠。
不知过了多少年，
大地人口骤然添。
因人皆食香土饱，
所食香土渐渐少。
为了方便觅香土，
八仙聚首又商讨。
认为东西与南北，
大地均分四洲好。

They had kept walking on and on.

It had been so long since they had parted

That they had forgotten about the agreement.

At last when they suddenly met,

The four immortals going west spoke first.

Thus they became women,

And those who went east continued to be men.

So the eight immortals became four couples,

And ever since then there was love among humans.

With the first four families,

Human beings began to multiply.

People then had no idea of time,

And time just went by.

Years and years had passed, and there was

A sharp increase in the population on the earth.

Because every person ate the fragrant soil,

It became less and less.

In order to search for more fragrant soil,

The eight immortals met again for a discussion.

They thought that the earth should be divided into four continents,

Conforming to the four directions: east, west, north and south.

四家各率儿孙齐,

各选一洲立根基。

大地从此始出现,

人间最初四聚落。

二

躲过天地劫火者,

即今人类之共祖。

彼于四方曼刚相①,

孕育繁兴诸民族。

最初南方曼刚相,

夫妇二人育二子。

次子即我德昂祖,

长成居于干补举②。

先祖于此生三子,

长子取名叫布朗③,

次子取名称别列④,

三子取名呼瓦弄⑤。

---

① 曼刚相:"曼"为村寨,"曼刚相"意为宝石中间的寨子。
② 干补举:德昂语,地域名,全称为"勐干补举",据说位于今天的柬埔寨。
③ 布朗:德昂语,据说就是今天的布朗族。
④ 别列:德昂语,又作"布龙",即德昂族。
⑤ 瓦弄:傣语,德昂语为"腊",据说就是今天的佤族。

The four families summoned all their children,

And each family chose a continent as their home base.

On the earth there began to appear

The first four clans of human settlements.

II

Those who survived the fire catastrophe

Were the ancestors of humans today.

They produced different clans of people

In the villages, called "Mangangxiang①", on the four continents.

In the first village on the southern continent,

The immortal couple bore two sons.

The second son was the forefather of the De'ang people,

Who grew up and went to live in Ganbuju②.

In that place our forefather bore three sons,

The eldest son was named Bulang③,

The second son was named Bielie④,

---

① Mangangxiang: "Man" means "village", and "mangangxiang" means a village surrounded with gemstones.
② Ganbuju: a De'ang term. The complete expression is "Meng Ganbuju". It is the name of a place located in today's Cambodia.
③ Bulang: In the De'ang language, it refers to the Bulang ethnic group in China.
④ Bielie: In the De'ang language, it's also written as "Bulong", referring to today's De'ang ethnic group.

父子兄弟和睦居，
繁衍生息渐兴荣。
而今德昂聪明智，
传统美德由此隆。
后辈儿孙应牢记，
代代相传勿忘本。
南方绿色干补举，
达古达楞源生地。

那时人间无四季，
气候温和宜人居。
那时无有星和月，
亦无昼夜相更替。
那时无有阳光照，
琅叨干帕耀大地。
那时只有风和雨，
因此人们岩洞居。
那时人们不穿衣，
因无严寒来相袭。
那时香土宜人年，
快乐无忧寿万千。

葫芦人的传说
The Legend of the Gourd People

And the third son was named Wanong[①].

Father and sons lived in harmony,

And their multiplication resulted in prosperity.

The De'ang people today are intelligent

Because they have inherited all of their traditional virtues.

Future generations should remember these virtues

And pass them on to your children and grandchildren.

This southern green village, Ganbuju,

Is the birthplace of Da-gu Da-leng.

In those days there were no seasons,

And the climate was mild and pleasant.

There were no stars or moon,

And there was no division between day and night.

There was no sun at that time.

The gourd shone over the earth.

There was only wind and rain,

So people lived in caves for shelter.

They didn't wear clothes,

For it was never cold.

There was plenty of fragrant soil to be healthy food,

---

① Wanong: a Dai term. In the De'ang language, it is pronounced "La", referring to today's Wa ethnic group.

可是好景即将逝，

人福渐薄情境迁。

由于人口剧然增，

岩洞已然不能容。

三子之父有神力，

大地之上织蛛网①。

他让儿孙出岩洞，

居于网下避雨风。

可是不久食物罄，

大地香土硬土同。

父亲愁得无一法，

只有祷求混西迦。

悲泪哀求九百次，

顿首又求九十九。

哭得双目泪成血，

求得开口声如裂。

混西迦被诚心动，

即刻招来混毕姐②。

混尚毕姐心地善，

承领天命解厄难。

---

① 蛛网：罗网，传说天界中有此罗网，其上装饰有无量珍宝。因为人们从来没有见过，于其形象极难想象，故将之形象地称为蛛网（蜘蛛网）。
② 混毕姐：混尚毕姐的简称，德昂族传说中主宰植物、果实的天神。

葫芦人的传说
The Legend of the Gourd People

And people lived long and happy.

But the good times were diminishing,

And the situation was deteriorating.

Because of the dramatic increase in population,

The caves were no longer spacious enough.

The father of the three sons had magical power

To spin vast spider webs① over the land.

He asked his children to move out of the caves

And take shelter from the rain and wind under the webs.

But soon there was no more fragrant soil,

Only hard earth.

The father grieved but found no solution,

So he had to pray to Emperor Hun Xijia for mercy.

He cried and pleaded with tears nine hundred times,

And then he kowtowed another ninety nine times.

He cried so sadly that his tears turned into blood,

And he prayed so hard that his voice became husky.

Emperor Hun Xijia was moved by his sincerity,

And instantly he summoned Hun Bijie②,

---

① Spider webs: Actually they refer to nets. Legend has it that in heaven there are nets decorated with pearls and other jewels. Humans have never seen them and could not imagine their appearance, so they called them spider webs.

② Hun Bijie: He is also called "Hun Shangbijie". According to the De'ang people's legends, he is the god in charge of plants and fruits.

他以天眼观人间，

人间果真绝了粮。

人间没有日月照，

人间没有星星亮。

只见一个宝葫芦，

搁置大地闪金光。

由于时久蒙尘土，

葫芦光彩渐暗淡。

看到人间此景象，

混尚毕姐心思量：

"如果人间无食粮，

人类如何能久长？

从来帕惹人间出，

人类若无缘何生？"

于是招来诸神仙，

一百零二齐集会。

混尚毕姐色庄严，

面对大家开了言：

"诸位仙人听我讲，

葫芦人的传说
The Legend of the Gourd People

Who was kindhearted
And willing to solve the problem.

He looked downward from heaven
And saw there was really no food on the earth.
There was neither a sun nor a moon shining,
And there were no twinkling stars.
He saw a precious gourd on the earth,
Which gave out golden light.
Because of the dust of years on it,
The gourd's luster had faded.
Seeing such scenes on the earth,
Hun Shangbijie thought to himself:
"If there is no food on the earth,
How can humans survive and live long?
Pare can be born only among humans.
If there is no human, how can he be born?"
Therefore he summoned all the deities for a meeting,
Which one hundred and two immortals attended.
Hun Shangbijie looked solemn.
He made a speech at the meeting:
"Let me tell you the truth:

如今人间断了粮。
粮食若无人类绝，
帕惹何能人间生。
我蒙天敕救世间，
还望诸位来相帮。
一百零二诸神仙，
谁愿下凡解灾殃？"
诸仙闻言皆欣愿，
个个愿速下凡间。
混尚毕姐心欢喜，
直飞九霄展翅羽。
陡然大风呼呼起，
骤然又落潇潇雨。
最后抖落身上羽，
数有一百又零二。
片片神羽各融入，
百位神仙之身躯。
一百神仙获神羽，
随即飘然下凡去。
不料尽随风雨转，
辗转无法到人间。

葫芦人的传说
The Legend of the Gourd People

Now the people on earth are running out of food.

People will become extinct if they lack food,

And then how can Pare be born among them?

I was assigned by the Emperor of Heaven to save the earth,

And I need your help.

We have one hundred and two immortals here,

And who will go down to the earth to stop the catastrophes?"

All the immortals were glad to go

Down to the earth immediately.

Hun Shangbijie felt relieved

And flew up into the air.

A sudden gust of wind rose,

And then a sudden spell of rain fell.

And finally he shook off the feathers from his body,

Which numbered one hundred and two.

The feathers blended into

The bodies of one hundred of the immortals.

Once the immortals were equipped with the feathers,

They flew toward the earth.

But they floated in the wind and rain,

And could not reach the earth.

此时只怪风雨急，
二仙蹉跎失神羽。
如此何能人间去，
只有再求混毕姐。
混尚毕姐把头摇，
神色黯然对其语：
"我身所有植物种，
皆付百仙带人间。
如今只剩茶树种，
时节未至怎给予。"
无奈二仙紧哀求，
只好前来求帕惹。
帕惹见了直摇头，
语混毕姐此事难。
混尚毕姐复哀求，
数满九千九百九。
又于尊前发誓愿，
粉身碎骨救人间。
守护人间四方神[①]，
亦齐来到齐祈求。

---

① 四方神：传说中的四大天王，俗称四大金刚。佛典中谓其居于欲界天最下层的四天王天，守护人间。

葫芦人的传说
The Legend of the Gourd People

Because the wind and rain was so heavy,

The other two immortals failed to catch the feathers,

Without which they could not reach the earth.

So they had to plead with Hun Bijie for help.

Hun Shangbijie shook his head

And said to them with a somber look:

"All the plant species I had

Were given to the one hundred immortals.

Now the only plant I have is tea,

But I have no tea seed to give you for this season.

But the two immortals kept begging,

So he had to go and beg Pare,

Who shook his head

And told Hun Bijie it was hard to get.

Hun Shangbijie pleaded again and again,

For nine thousand nine hundred and ninety times.

Then he made a vow before Pare

That he would devote his life to saving mankind.

The four guardian gods[①] whose mission was protecting the earth

Also came to plead with Pare.

---

① Four guardian gods: They are also called "four guardian warriors". In the Buddhist scriptures they live in the lowest layer of Heaven and their duty is to guard the human world.

帕惹内心暗称叹，
赞彼救世心意坚。
于是手出七叶宝，
金银玉叶各七片。

宝叶付予混毕姐，
天空大地齐震动。
帕惹颜慈色光明，
殷勤咐嘱混毕姐：
"混尚毕姐行难行，
救世重任担在肩。
故应将此七叶宝，
二十一叶融彼身。
如此直至舍身命，
救世心愿定实现。"
混尚毕姐闻此言，
泪流满面心欢喜。
顷刻手中七叶宝，
化为香光融于身。

再说天帝混西迦，
本是天上领头人。

Pare was happy to see all this

And praised them for their strong desire to save the world.

Then he took out the seven-leaf treasure with

Seven pieces of gold, seven pieces of silver and seven pieces of jade.

When the seven-leaf treasure was handed to Hun Bijie,

The sky and the earth shook.

Pare's face was bright with kindness,

And he said to Hun Bijie warm-heartedly:

"You are going to do a very hard job,

Shouldering the burden of saving the world.

Therefore, the twenty-one leaves of the treasures

Should be absorbed into your body.

This will continue until you sacrifice your life,

And salvation will surely come true."

When Hun Shangbijie heard this,

Tears of joy streamed down his face.

In an instant the seven-leaf treasure in his hand

Was absorbed into his body.

Let's come back to the Emperor of Heaven Hun Xijia,

Who was the leader of Heaven.

彼命四方四天神，

精勤守护于人间。

四神又派众善神，

护持人间无懈怠。

从此人间就有了，

地水火风四灵气。

灵气又化为四神，

四神皆名布阿婆①。

彼与众神齐聚首，

要为人间来计议：

"认为人间无日月，

琅叨干帕久蒙尘。

彼之光明渐暗淡，

人间不久成黑暗

如此人类怎生活，

如此众神尽失职。

因此应向上天祈，

日月齐临照人间。"

于是一起返四天，

向四天神齐哀求。

四神摆手又摇头，

---

① 布阿婆：德昂族传说中守护人间的四位善神，分别由地、水、火、风四大元素之精华所化现，属较之天神地位略低的地神一类，归四方天神所统领。

He demanded the four guardian gods

To diligently protect the human world.

The four gods in turn asked all the good gods

To protect the world diligently.

Because of this, there were

Four elements, earth, water, fire and wind, in the world.

These four elements finally turned into four deities,

Who shared the same name, god of mercy[①].

These four gods met with the other gods and immortals,

And they had a discussion about the problems concerning the earth:

"There is no sun or moon over the earth,

And the gourd has long been covered with thick dust.

So the light of the gourd has been fading

And soon the human world will be entirely dark.

In that case humans cannot continue to live,

And that would be a considerable dereliction of duty by all of us gods.

So we must plead to the Emperor of Heaven

And ask that the sun and the moon shine over the earth."

Together they went to the four directions of heaven

And pleaded to the four gods in charge of the four directions.

---

① God of mercy: The four gods of mercy are called "Buapo" in the De'ang language. According to the De'ang legends, they are the incarnations of the essence of the four elements, earth, water, fire and wind, and their position is a bit lower than the four guardian gods, who therefore are their superiors.

皆云不会造日月。
众神又求混西迦,
天帝也说不会造。
于是天帝领众神,
帕惹尊前来祈求。
帕惹慈悲色庄严,
告彼此事不须忧。
日月还有众星辰,
已然交付混毕姐。
天帝闻说心欢喜,
转而相告混毕姐。

再说百仙下人间,
尚有二仙滞于天。
二仙唯恐赶不上,
先下人间一百仙。
于是复向混毕姐,
九千九百九次求。
混尚毕姐无他法,
意欲舍身为人间。
先向二仙传咒语,

The Legend of the Gourd People

The four gods shook their heads and waved their hands,

Saying they were unable to create a sun or a moon.

The gods turned to Hun Xijia, the emperor of Heaven,

But the Emperor of Heaven also said he couldn't do it.

Then he led the deities

To Pare and pleaded for his help.

Pare, merciful and solemn,

Told them not to worry about it.

As for the sun and the moon and the stars,

He had asked Hun Bijie to handl it.

The Emperor of Heaven was glad to hear that

And told Hun Bijie about it.

Let's return to the descending of these immortals to the earth,

Two of whom returned to heaven for help.

They were afraid they could not

Catch up with the other one hundred.

So they again pleaded with Hun Bijie

Nine thousand nine hundred and nine times.

Hun Shangbijie had no choice

But to devote himself to saving the creatures on the earth.

First he taught some incantations to the two immortals,

又剐身肉付二仙。

二仙见状齐悲泣,

无奈遵敕下凡间。

二仙喃喃持咒语,

狂风骤雨呼呼起。

先将两人各吹散,

又将两人拢一起。

风吹一仙昏迷去,

醒来变成漂亮女。

由于此时力将尽,

辗转无法飘落地。

另外一仙力量大,

最先飘落勐高棉[①]。

落地化为英俊男,

与空中女遥相望。

靓妹空中声声唤,

俊哥地上急急呼。

眼看风送人渐远,

即将飘回天庭去。

哥哥急得肝肠断,

忙将仙藤绕成圈。

---

① 勐高棉:地名,意为像蜘蛛网一样所覆盖的地方。德昂族人认为其位于今天的柬埔寨一带。

葫芦人的传说
The Legend of the Gourd People

And then cut off his flesh for them.

The two immortals saw it and wept,

But they had to obey the order to go to the earth.

They murmured the incantations,

And all of a sudden a storm broke out,

Blowing them apart

And bringing them together again.

One immortal lost consciousness during the storm

And became a beautiful woman when he came to.

Because she was exhausted,

She could not land herself.

The other was strong

And landed in Mon Khmer①.

He turned into a handsome man,

Looking at the woman far away in the sky.

The beautiful woman in the sky repeatedly called out to him,

And the handsome man on the earth worriedly called back.

The wind was about to blow the woman back to heaven.

The man was so anxious and heart-broken

That he twisted a magic rattan piece into a loop

And flung it into the sky.

---

① Mon Khmer: It means a place covered with something like spider webs. The De'ang people believe it to be located in today's Cambodia.

达古达楞格莱标 // Da-gu Da-leng Gelaibiao

藤圈极力天上抛,
箍住妹腰落地上。
从此二人结双对,
女弱于男源于此。
因此若人讨媳妇,
令缠腰箍才可靠。

彼见人间无所有,
百仙尚未到人间。
于是念咒向天吹,
百仙这才落人间。
百仙落地即变成,
九千万类之植物。
混尚毕姐身血肉,
途中风雨吹落散。
血点飞空化星辰,
从此天空繁星亮。
肉碎落地即变成,
九千万类陆动物。
自剐血肉混毕姐,
此时只剩骨架身。
由于吃了七叶宝,

葫芦人的传说
The Legend of the Gourd People

It caught the woman by the waist

And brought her down to the ground.

From then on they lived as a married couple.

That's why women today are weaker than men.

So if a man wants to marry a woman,

He must make a waist-band to hold her tight.

The man saw that there was nothing on the earth,

As the other hundred immortals had not yet arrived.

So he murmured an incantation and blew it into the air,

Which brought the hundred immortals to the ground.

Once the hundred immortals landed on the earth,

They turned into ninety million species of plants.

The flesh and blood of Hun Shangbijie

Had been scattered by the storm in the sky.

Blood drops turned into stars,

Which since that time have twinkled in the sky.

His flesh pieces fell to the ground

And turned into ninety million terrestrial animals.

Because he had cut his flesh and blood for mankind,

He only had a skeleton left.

But because he had the seven-leaf treasure in his body,

全身处处成利益。
心脏变成了太阳,
头骨飘空成月亮。
从此人间日月临,
从此人间现光明。
混尚毕姐欲令人,
知其曾为植物主。
于是从鼻生长出,
一棵苍苍大茶树。
今人若睹夜明月,
尚可见此茶树王。
混尚毕姐身筋络,
化为人间各种藤。
身上毛发亦化为,
人间五谷与百草。
混尚毕姐身血脉,
化作人间江河流。
余骨落水就变成,
十千万类水动物。
倾尽一切混毕姐,

The Legend of the Gourd People

Every part of his body became a treasure.

His heart became the sun,

And his skull turned into the moon.

From that day on,

The sun and the moon have shone over the earth,

And there is light in the world.

Hun Shangbijie wished people on the earth

To know that he was the lord of all plants,

So out of his nose

Grew a huge green tea tree.

If one looks carefully at the bright moon at night,

He will be able to see this huge tea tree.

The muscles of Hun Shangbijie

Turned into the various vines.

His hair turned into

Grain and all kinds of grass.

His arteries and veins

Turned into rivers flowing around the earth.

His bones fell into the water

And turned into many kinds of aquatic animals.

After every part of his body was put into use,

神魂化作体令噶①。

从此人间现生机，

从此人间衣食足。

三

人间虽复现生机，

大地物产亦丰足。

然而此时人天真，

生餐体露识未开。

此时人寿亦久长，

人与天神一处居。

洛体令噶空中飞，

来去往返千百回。

为护人间勤巡察，

为益人类示神变。

彼至人们觅食地，

变现一头大白象。

人见白象齐聚首，

---

① 体令噶：又叫洛体令噶。德昂族传说中守护人间的神鸟，为主宰植物的天神混尚毕姐之神魂所化，体形巨大，能长时飞行。其与传说中的大鹏鸟是否为同一种鸟，尚不能确定。

葫芦人的传说
The Legend of the Gourd People

His soul turned into Tilingga[①].

Ever since that time life had returned to the human world,

And humans have been well fed and clothed.

III

Life had returned to the human world,

And the earth was abundant with natural resources.

But humans of that time were naive.

They ate raw food, wore no clothes, and had no knowledge.

They enjoyed long lives

And lived with the immortals.

Luotilingga flew back and forth in the air

Thousands of times.

To protect humans he went on patrol,

To benefit mankind he underwent metamorphosis.

Once he flew to where humans looked for food,

He changed into a white elephant.

Seeing the animal, the humans got together

---

① Tilingga: a divine bird, also called Luotilingga. According to the De'ang legends, this divine bird is the incarnation of the soul of Hun Shangbijiie, the god of plants and fruits. The divine bird, huge in size and good at flying, was born to protect the human world.

欲猎此象做食物。
棍石铁块齐向彼,
铁石交击火星迸。
火星点燃干茸草,
从此人们知用火。
有人持竹去猎象,
不意竹裂划手破。
试用茅草竹上拭,
茅草立断成两截。
始知锋利人堪用,
从此人类知用刀。
人见鸟于巢内居,
能避寒冷与风雨。
便采茅草覆枝头,
从此人们知建房。
那时人们身赤露,
只用树叶稍蔽体。
后见兽皮晒干后,
保暖遮风又牢实。
便用细藤相连结,
从此人们始穿衣。

The Legend of the Gourd People

And decided to kill it for food.

Sticks, stones and iron chunks were all thrown at it,

Producing flying sparks,

Which ignited the dry grass.

From then on people knew how to make fire.

Some used bamboo to hit the elephant,

And the bamboo split and wounded their hands.

They rubbed cogon grass on the split bamboo,

And it was cut into two pieces.

Thus they knew that sharp objects were useful,

And began to make and use knives.

When humans saw that birds lived in nests

To protect themselves from cold and wind and rain,

They learned to build houses

By covering the trees with thatch.

At that time people were naked:

They only covered their bodies with a few leaves.

Later they found that after animals' skins were dried,

They were useful to keep the body warm.

They connected the skins with vines.

This was how they started to make and wear clothes.

时人居洞已长久,
人丁兴旺渐拥塞。
于是人渐离岩洞,
水边林下茅棚居。
然而谁也不能忘,
陡峭岩壁之石洞。
"陡峭岩壁"德昂语,
呼作"雅昂"人皆知。
以后不论迁何所,
皆云我从雅昂来。
时久渐呼成"德昂",
德昂遂成我族名。
原之族名"勐高棉",
日久渐渐无人晓。

那时不分日与夜,
那时无有四季交。
寒暑往来律度失,
风施雨行无节令。
日出便无风和雨,
风雨若至无日出。
雨时四处洪水涨,

The Legend of the Gourd People

Humans had lived in caves for a long time,

And the increase of population found the caves crowded.

So they began to leave the caves

And lived under thatched huts by the rivers.

But they never forgot

The caves on steep cliffs.

Steep cliffs had a name in the De'ang language,

And that was "ya'ang".

Later no matter where they moved,

They all said they moved from Ya'ang.

As time went on, it sounded more like "De'ang",

And De'ang became the name of our ethnic group.

The original clan name "Mon Khmer"

Was gradually replaced and forgotten.

At that time there was no division of day and night,

Nor was there any division of seasons.

The change between summer and winter was irregular,

And wind and rain followed no seasonal pattern.

There was no wind or rain when the sun was out,

And there was no sunshine when there was wind or rain.

When it rained, floods arose everywhere,

晴则酷日裂大地。

因无节令束气候，

树木百草失荣色。

加之人口日渐多，

食物供给倍艰难。

于是人群意见生，

大事小事吵不休。

最终族群一分三，

一留原地二迁移。

一群迁至勐混敏①，

一群迁徒至勐果②。

此时四方四天神，

地水火风布阿婆。

看到人间无节令，

处境艰难生活惨。

于是相约到天庭，

禀报天帝混西迦。

天帝闻奏即招来，

日神月神风雨神。

---

① 勐混敏：地名，意为会飞男人居住的地方。可能位于今天的大理洱海一带，也有说就在今天的昆明滇池周围。
② 勐果：地名，据传诵者言，勐果就是今天的蒙古。

葫芦人的传说
The Legend of the Gourd People

And when it was sunny, the heat burnt the land.

Because there was no seasonal climate,

Trees and grass withered.

Due to the growing population,

The food supply became harder and harder maintain.

Thus people began to divide in opinions

And quarreled over major or minor matters.

Finally the clan was divided into three branches,

One branch stayed while the other two migrated,

One to Meng Hunmin[①],

The other to Meng Guo[②].

Now let's return to the four guardian gods

And the four gods of mercy.

They saw there were no regular seasons on the earth,

And human life was difficult and full of tragedy.

So they met again and decided

To report this to the Emperor of Heaven, Hun Xijia,

Who immediately summoned

The sun god, the moon god, the wind god and the rain god.

---

① Meng Hunmin: It means a place where flying people live. It's said to be located either in the Erhai lake area of Dali or the Dianchi lake area of Kunming.
② Meng Guo: a place said to be today's Mongolia.

达古达楞格莱标 // Da-gu Da-leng Gelaibiao

众神聚齐来商量，

要让人间有节令。

四方天神向天帝，

躬身作礼先开言：

"今后日月昼夜替，

每天二六时辰交。

一年具足十二月，

一月共有三十天。

一年三季来交换，

一季总共有四月①。

风雨冷暖循规律，

如此节令宜人间。"

四布阿婆闻此言，

起身忙对大家说：

"四位天神法虽好，

然有少分不合理。

若十二月为一年，

---

① 一季四月：在德昂族使用的历法（德昂语为"冷唐"，即佛历）中，将一年分为三季，一季分为四个月。

葫芦人的传说
The Legend of the Gourd People

The gods came together for a discussion and decided

That there should be regular seasons on the earth.

The four guardian gods of heaven

Bowed before the Emperor of Heaven and said,

"The sun and the moon will alternate between day and night.

The shift will occur at six in the morning and in the evening.

One year will include twelve months,

And each month will have thirty days.

One year will include three seasons,

And one season will have four months①.

Wind, rain, cold and warmth will come regularly.

This division of seasons is good for mankind."

Hearing this, the four gods of mercy

Got up and said,

"The solution of the four guardian gods is good,

But there are some defects.

If one year is divided into twelve months,

---

① A season should include four months: In De'ang people's traditional calendar, which is a Buddhist calendar, a year is divided into three seasons and a season includes four months.

大中小年①应分明。

年月有闰居何时，

月大月小应分清。"

四方天神闻言后，

神色傲慢心不喜。

认为天神地位高，

懂得定比地神多。

彼仅人间布阿婆，

怎敢说我不合理。

于是出言强相辩，

敢以砍头为赌注。

四布阿婆心坦然，

因彼身俱四灵气②。

不畏天威据理争，

砍头相胁亦不惊。

双方如此争不休，

谁也不肯把错认。

---

① 大中小年：在德昂族使用的历法中，有大年、中年和小年之分。一年十二个月中，单月（即一、三、五、七、九、十一月）各有二十九天，双月（即二、四、六、八、十、十二月）各有三十天，此谓之小年；一年十二月中，六月、七月、八月各三十天，其余月份天数与小年相同，此谓之中年；一年十二月中，六月、七月、八月、闰八月各有三十天，其余月份天数与小年相同，此谓之大年。

② 四灵气：佛教认为，物理世界是由地、水、火、风四种元素构成。此处"四灵气"即指地、水、火、风四大种性精华之气。

葫芦人的传说

The Legend of the Gourd People

There should be a distinction between big, medium and small years①.

Leap years and leap months should be decided,

And big months and small months should be specified."

When the four guardian gods heard this,

They had arrogant looks and became unhappy.

They thought, as gods in heaven, they had greater authority

Knew more than the four gods of mercy from the earth,

Who were just gods of the human world

And had no right to disagree with them.

So they stubbornly challenged the four gods of mercy.

To bet their heads on the matter.

The four gods of mercy were not frightened

Because they embodied the four elements②.

Defying the four gods from heaven,

They took their own stance, fearing no death.

---

① Big, medium and small years: In the De'ang calendar, there are big, medium and small years. In a small year, there are 29 days in each odd month (January, March, May, July, September and November) and 30 days in each even month (February, April, June, August, October and December) ; In a medium year, there are 29 days in each odd month except July (January, March, May, September and November) and 30 days in each even month plus July (February, April, June, July, August, October and December) ; In a big year, there are 29 days in each odd month except July (January, March, May, September and November) and 30 days in each even month plus July and Leap August (February, April, June, July, August, October and December).

② The four elements: Buddhists believe that the physical world is composed of four elements – earth, water, fire and wind. The four gods absorbed the essence of the four elements.

只好彼此相约定，
共请天帝来作证：
人间节气先按照，
四方天神计划行。
若谁方法行不通，
就要砍断谁方头。
再说人间之节气，
四方天神法先行。
最初风调雨也顺，
人类生活亦安康。
可是好景不长久，
数年以后起灾殃。
冬季大雨止不住，
洪水泛滥生灵苦。
夏季无雨烈日酷，
瘟疫肆虐尸骨遍。
观见此景混西迦，
急忙招来各路仙。
人间节令命调整，
换做布阿婆法行。
从此人间风雨顺，
从此人间节令调。

葫芦人的传说
The Legend of the Gourd People

The two sides were so divided

That no side would give in.

They had to agree with each other

To invite the Emperor of Heaven to be the arbiter:

The seasons in the human world

Would first follow the four guardian gods' plan.

No matter whose plan failed,

Their heads would be cut off.

So the seasons in the human world

First followed the four guardian gods' plan.

At the beginning, the weather was favorable,

And people enjoyed a comfortable life.

But it didn't last long,

Because a few years later, disaster struck.

The winter rains would not stop,

And the people were afflicted with floods.

In summer, there was no rain and the sun burned hot,

And plagues raged and resulted in a lot of deaths.

Seeing this, Hun Xijia, the Emperor of Heaven,

Summoned all the immortals and gods.

He asked them to adjust the seasons

Using the plan of the four gods of mercy.

此时天帝混西迦，
语四天神布阿婆：
"尔等双方曾赌誓，
邀我为尔作证人。
如今对错已分明，
此案今日应了结。"
四天①闻说心惭愧，
躬身作礼齐开言：
"从来天神最正直，
真诚守信表人天。
既有誓约言在先，
我等认错甘断首。"
于是就有大力神，
各持刀斧砍其头。
可是无论怎么砍，
四天头无毫发损。
再借四天宝刀砍，
其首亦难损分毫。
无奈往询四天妻，
四天神妻倍为难。
怕露秘密夫受苦，

---

① 四天：四方天神，亦即四大天王。

葫芦人的传说
The Legend of the Gourd People

Now the weather was fine

And the seasons were normal.

The Emperor of Heaven

Said to the two groups of gods,

"You two had a bet,

And asked me to be the arbiter.

Now that the outcome is clear,

The case should come to a close today."

Feeling ashamed, the four gods①

Bowed and said,

"We who come from heaven are always upright

And keep our promises as an example for others.

Since we have lost the bet,

We are ready to have our heads cut off."

Then there came four gods of strength,

And each held an axe and tried to cut one head.

But however hard they tried, they could

Do no damage to the heads of the four convicted gods.

They used the four gods' own swords instead,

But again no damage was heone.

Helplessly they consulted the wives of the four gods,

---

① The four gods: the four guardian gods.

不告又恐众神讥。
毕竟四天非凡人，
纵砍彼头亦不死。
利弊数数相权衡，
终将秘密来相告：
"各路神仙听我言，
我等夫君神通大。
任尔何法难害彼，
唯我发能断其头。"
闻得此言大力神，
立刻跪求彼发丝。
四天神妻各拔下，
发丝一根予众神。
发丝做成发丝弓，
轻易割下四天首。

四天首级才割下，
首级突然起大火。
熊熊大火炽且盛，
即将来把天界烧。

葫芦人的传说
The Legend of the Gourd People

Who were in a dilemma.

If they revealed the secret, their husbands would suffer.

If not, they might be laughed at by other gods.

After all, as immortals, the four gods

Wouldn't die even if their heads were cut off.

Weighing the pros and cons,

The wives revealed the secret,

"Gods and immortals,

Our husbands have magic power.

Whatever weapons you use, you cannot hurt them.

Only our hairs can break their heads.

Hearing this, the gods of strength

Immediately knelt down to beg for hairs.

The four wives each pulled out a hair

And gave it to the gods of strength.

Each hair was made into a bow,

Which easily cut off the heads of the four gods.

The four heads burst into flames

As soon as they were cut off.

The blazing fire became so strong

That it would soon burn heaven.

众神将头急埋地，
大地顷刻巨火燃。
眼看人间之生灵，
将遭涂炭尽无余。
又将首级速扔海，
大海又变巨火海。
众神谁也没料到，
四天头颇成祸害。
大家只好又商量，
如何安放四天首。
思来想去无良策，
只有再求四天妻。
四天有妻各七位，
个个美丽又贤淑。
彼等答应众神请，
每天轮流抱夫头。
四天头方入妻怀，
熊熊巨火遽然灭。
如此一天又一天，
这样一年复一年。
天上一天人一载，
二十八妻轮流抱。

葫芦人的传说
The Legend of the Gourd People

The gods hurriedly buried the heads in the ground,

But in an instant the earth was on fire.

Seeing that the living things of the world

Would all soon be burned to a crisp,

They threw the heads into the sea,

But the sea instantly became a huge fire.

None of the gods expected

That these heads would become a disaster.

They had to meet again for a resolution

On how to deal with the four heads.

Having no ideas,

They had to turn again to the wives of the four gods.

Each of the four gods had seven wives,

All of whom were beautiful and virtuous.

The wives promised to the gods that they would

Take turns to hold their husbands' heads every day.

As soon as the heads were placed in the wives' hands,

The fires died down.

It went on day after day

And year after year.

One day in heaven was one year on the earth.

The twenty-eight wives took turns holding the heads.

四天神首已然断,
众神各各心难安。
于是天帝携众神,
往诣四天与其妻。
四天神妻眼含泪,
一齐开口语众神:
"我夫尊首虽然断,
然而身命却不死。
天上人间许多事,
尚待四天为料理。
故而请求混西迦,
找来他首接夫头。"
天帝闻言忙允诺,
敕令众神四方寻。
北方找来大象首,
南方寻得黄牛头。
东方遍觅获猪首,
西方访求得马头。
于是众神将四首,
一一接作四天头。
从此四天现畜首,

葫芦人的传说
The Legend of the Gourd People

The gods felt sorry

That the heads of the four gods had been cut off,

So the Emperor of Heaven took all the gods

To visit the wives of the four gods.

Tears in their eyes,

The wives said to the visitors,

"Our husbands' heads have been cut off,

But their bodies are still alive.

Many problems in heaven and on earth

Are waiting for them to find a solution.

So we want to ask the Emperor of Heaven

To find heads to put onto our husbands' bodies."

The Emperor of Heaven gave them his promise.

He demanded all the gods to look for four heads.

The head of an elephant was found in the north,

The head of a ox was found in the south,

The head of a pig was found in the east,

And the head of a horse was found in the west.

Then the gods brought back the four heads

And connected them to the headless bodies.

Since then, the four guardian gods with animal heads

继为人天做守护。

传说南方之天神，

因为接了黄牛首。

至今南方喝水人，

咽水喉皆出"哦"音。

自从斩去四天首，

又割人间四畜头。

天帝惶惶心不安，

担心有罪不能酬。

于是找来布阿婆，

虚心下问有罪否？

四布阿婆齐作礼，

将诚实言告天帝：

"陛下先斩四天首，

又许众神割畜头。

此罪业因已成立，

业果熟时苦当受。"①

天帝闻说心忧惧，

---

① 业因、业果：佛教将人的行为、语言和思想的造作称为三业，行善、语善、心善为三善业，反之为三恶业。三善业为因感生乐果，三恶业为因感生苦果。此善恶之因的造作到苦乐之果的成熟随缘发现，犹如车轮，因能感果，果又为因，循环往复，无有止尽，能通于过去、现在、未来之三世，此称之为业因和业果。

葫芦人的传说
The Legend of the Gourd People

Continued their duty of guarding heaven and the people of the earth.

Legend has it that because the god guarding the south

Had the head of the ox,

The throats of southerners give out an "oh" sound

When they drink water.

After the heads of the four gods were cut off,

Four heads of animals were also cut off.

That worried the Emperor of Heaven a lot,

Since he feared that he was sinful and would not be blessed.

So he summoned the four gods of mercy

And asked them whether he was guilty or not.

The four gods of mercy saluted him

And told him the truth,

"Your Majesty first had the heads of the four guardian gods cut off,

And then allowed the gods to behead the animals.

The sin has been committed,

急问何法罪可弭。
四布阿婆再作礼，
将灭罪法告天帝：
"陛下息心听我言，
臣有良策罪可弭。
二十八位天神妻，
为抱夫首交相替。
每天相互交接时，
血迹皆用圣水洗。
此时正值人世间，
每年清明后十天。
陛下可救人世间，
每年清明之此时，
亦用人间浴佛水，
相互泼洒除邪浊。
如此就能弭陛下，
命斩四天之罪愆。
大象黄牛与猪马，
无量恩德人感念。
由于献出自己头，
人间得以免灾殃。
陛下可救人世间，

And you will suffer from its consequence in due time."①

The Emperor of Heaven was frightened

And asked how to avoid punishment.

The four gods of mercy bowed again,

And told him how,

"Your Majesty, don't worry.

We have a good idea for you.

Those twenty-eight wives of the four guardian gods

Take turns to hold their husbands' heads.

Every day when they change shifts,

They use holy water to wash away the blood.

The time they change shifts in heaven happens to be

Ten days after the Tomb-Sweeping Day on the earth.

Your Majesty may order the people of the world

On the Tomb-Sweeping Day every year

To sprinkle Pare's bathwater

Over each other so as to wash away evil things.

---

① The sin and its consequence: They are also called "Karma" in Buddhism. Buddhism refers to the effect of human behavior, language, and thought as the three karma, and good behavior, kind words and kind hearts are considered to be the Three Good Karma, and their opposites are called the Three Evil Karma. The three good karma bring about good consequence, and the three evil karma are the cause of suffering. The relationship between the formation of the good and evil causes and the maturity of the effects of bitterness and pleasure is discovered to be like a wheel, where the cause can sense the effect, and the effect is the cause. It goes on and on. Such causes and effects of the three karma are interconnected within three life circles – past, present and future. These are called the sin and its consequence.

将彼四畜骨焚化。

如此就可弭陛下,

许割畜头之过愆。"

天帝闻言心欢喜,

即刻敕令依法行。

从此人间就有了,

一年一度泼水节。

从此人间就实行,

一年一度吉美蹦①。

---

① 吉美蹦:德昂语,俗称"烧白柴",傣语称为"索顺诺",为德昂族和傣族共同的节日。德昂族在"冷唐"历("冷唐"系德昂语,即佛历)每年三月十四、十五日举行,傣族在傣历每年四月十四、十五日举行,约为农历的正月中旬。每到这个时候,德昂族家家户户都要到山上砍来一种特定的树木,将树皮剥去,再把净裸如白骨般的树干供献到佛寺,集中堆砌呈塔状,再由佛爷或村长老主持仪式,举火焚烧,以此纪念为四位天神献出头颅的象、牛、猪、马四种动物。

葫芦人的传说
The Legend of the Gourd People

In this way, Your Majesty can erase

Your sin of having the four guardian gods' heads cut off.

As for the elephant, the ox, the pig and the horse,

People are grateful to them for their great sacrifice.

By contributing their heads,

They helped the human world exorcise disaster.

Your Majesty may order the people

To burn the bones of the four animals.

In this way, Your Majesty can be pardoned

For cutting off the heads of the four animals."

The Emperor of Heaven rejoiced of those words

And immediately gave orders for these things to be carried out.

Ever since then,

There is an annual Water-Sprinkling Festival.

And ever since then,

There is a Jimeibeng Festival[1] in the human world.

---

[1] Jimeibeng Festival: It's a De'ang term, commonly known as "burning white wood" and the Dai term is "Suoshunnuo". It is a common festival for the De'ang and the Dai people. The De'ang people celebrate the festival on March 14th and 15th each year according to their Buddhist calendar Leng Tang ("Leng Tang" is a De'ang term for "Buddhist calendar") and the Dai people celebrate the festival on April 14th and 15th each year, which is the middle of the first lunar month of a year. Every year at this time, every De'ang family would go to the mountain to cut down a specific tree, peel off its bark, and then offer the naked bone-like trunks to the Buddhist temple. All the trunks are then piled into the shape of a pagoda. Then the abbot of the temple or the village head would host the ceremony and set fire to the trunk pile to commemorate the four animals—elephant, ox, pig, and horse that gave their heads to the four guardian gods.

茶树、粮种和衣饰的来历
The Origin of Tea Trees, Grain Seeds and Clothes

达古达楞格莱标 // Da-gu Da-leng Gelaibiao

一

茶树来由不平凡，
混尚毕姐恩情长。
先将骨肉洒大地，
人间才有食物享。
又将心首化日月，
人间才能光明亮。
粉身碎骨为人类，
无比恩德怎能忘！
此后德昂凡修善，
功德皆分彼一半。

再说殁后混毕姐，
身虽消散神不灭。
因为救世心愿大，
魂神化作体令噶。
空中日日勤巡视，
人间岁岁做护持。
一日因为渴得紧，
于是飞临河边饮。

茶树、粮种和衣饰的来历
The Origin of Tea Trees, Grain Seeds and Clothes

I

The origin of tea trees has an extraordinary legend,

Thanks to Hun Shangbijie, god of plants and fruits.

He first scattered his flesh and bones onto the earth,

So that there was food for humans.

Then his heart and head turned into the sun and the moon,

So that there was light in the human world.

Every part of his body was given to human beings.

How can we forget his incomparable kindness!

Ever since then whenever a good deed is done,

Half of the merit is owed to him.

After Hun Bijie died,

His body had dissipated but his soul didn't perish.

Because his wish to save the world was so great,

His soul was transformed into Tilingga,

Which patrolled the earth day after day

And protected the world year after year.

One day the divine bird was so thirsty

That he flew to the river to drink.

达古达楞格莱标 // Da-gu Da-leng Gelaibiao

由于渴急喝不止，
不意却被水撑死。
呜呼悲叹人福薄，
人间守护轻易殁。

彼时崃弄①有国王，
王母由疾双目盲。
膝下唯有一公主，
美丽善良又贤淑。
攀亲俊彦过千百，
求亲贵胄八方来。
可是公主不寻常，
权贵财势看不上。
偏偏爱个穷伙计，
招赘做了王女婿。
穷小伙子名姐苏②，
据说来自日出处。
他有夙愿在心间，
访仙寻宝到天边。
再三征得王同意，

---

① 崃弄：地名，意为大山，位于今天缅甸的北部。
② 姐苏：全称"阿銮姐苏"，许多德昂族传诵者认为，姐苏是一名汉族神仙。

茶树、粮种和衣饰的来历
The Origin of Tea Trees, Grain Seeds and Clothes

Unfortunately, he died

From drinking too much water.

The people were sad

That their guardian had died so easily.

At that time there was a kingdom named Lainong[①],

And the queen of the kingdom was blind from disease.

The king and the queen had a princess,

She was beautiful, kind and virtuous.

Hundreds of handsome guys wished to marry her,

And nobles from all over the world proposed to her.

But the princess was unusual,

Who despised the rich and the powerful.

She fell in love with a poor young man

And married him in the palace.

The young man was named Jiesu[②], who was said

To have come from the place where the sun rose.

He had an old wish in his heart, wanted

To visit the immortals and look for treasure.

After he got permission from the king,

---

① Lainong: It's the name of a place, meaning a big mountain, and it is located in the northern part of Myanmar.
② Jiesu: a man's name and the full name is "Aluan Jiesu". Many De'ang narrators believe that he is a Han fairy.

达古达楞格莱标 // Da-gu Da-leng Gelaibiao

含泪惜别新婚妻。
然后带着五百属,
离开王宫上旅途。
可是谁也不知道,
天边路程有多少?
大家向着日出方,
走过万水与千山。
某日行至一河边,
河水汹涌浪滔天。
姐苏见状命从者,
伐木扎筏以渡河。

话说天上混西迦,
人间本其主宰下。
曾于劫火来临前,
将巨宝藏藏天边。
不知过去几多时,
天帝秘密无人知。
这次眼看穷姐苏,
过河就到藏宝处。
人类贪心无足厌,
世上无如人欲险。

茶树、粮种和衣饰的来历
The Origin of Tea Trees, Grain Seeds and Clothes

He tearfully waved goodbye to his new wife.

Then, followed by five hundred companions,

He left the palace and embarked on his journey.

But no one knew

How far it was from the palace to the edge of the earth.

They traveled towards the place where the sun rose up,

Crossing thousands of rivers and mountains.

One day they arrived at a river,

Which was raging and turbulent with high waves.

Jiesu asked his followers

To cut down trees and make boats.

Hun Xijia, the Emperor of Heaven,

Under whose rule was the human world,

Hid the great treasure at the edge of the earth

Before the fire catastrophe broke out.

Numerous years had passed,

But the secret of the treasure remained unknown.

Now the poor man Jiesu would approach it

Once he crossed the river.

Human greed was insatiable.

Nothing was more dangerous than human greed.

宝藏如果被发现，

贻害无穷在人间。

天帝心急似火燃，

急携王母①下了凡。

变作公公老奶奶，

齐向姐苏走过来。

问姐苏等何处去，

伐木造筏何方趋？

姐苏答云欲渡河，

去做云乡天边客。

公公听了急摆手，

奶奶听了便摇头。

公公要把原委述，

奶奶抢着告姐苏：

"那时我俩也年轻，

妙龄十六成的亲。

我俩婚前发誓言，

要到天边访神仙。

婚后一月就出发，

携手行路往天涯。

艰难困苦都尝尽，

---

① 王母：汉族民间称之为"王母娘娘"，乃天帝混西迦（玉皇大帝）的妻子。

茶树、粮种和衣饰的来历
The Origin of Tea Trees, Grain Seeds and Clothes

If the treasure was found,

It would do limitless harm to the world.

The Emperor of Heaven was so worried

That he went down to the earth with his queen[①].

They changed into an old man and an old woman

And walked up to Jiesu.

They asked him where he and his companions were heading for,

And where they were going by boat.

Jiesu replied that they wanted to cross the river

In order to visit a place at the edge of the earth.

At that, the old man waved his hand

And the old woman shook her head.

The old man was just about to tell the truth

When the old woman said in haste,

"When we two were young,

We got married at the age of sixteen.

We vowed before marriage

That we would visit the gods at the edge of the earth.

So we set off a month after our marriage,

Hand in hand we went to the ends of the earth.

Though we had gone through all kinds of difficulties,

---

① Queen of Heaven: The Han people call her "Her Majesty Queen of Heaven", and she is the wife of the Emperor of Heaven Hun Xijia (the Jade Emperor).

我俩始终不变心。
可是漫漫天涯路，
悠悠不见终尽处。
如此即便尽形寿，
亦无法到天尽头。
无奈只好把心死，
悻悻回头往家走。
至今龄近九十九，
一生兼程无停留。
你我今日幸有缘，
不期此地得遇见。
奉劝你等后生辈，
赶快洗心听我言。
前路漫漫多恶鬼，
虎狼当道太凶险。
我俩后尘万莫步，
快快回头莫少住。"
姐苏闻说久无言，
无奈接受二老劝。
他请二老在先归，
自率众人于后随。
于是天帝携王母，

茶树、粮种和衣饰的来历
The Origin of Tea Trees, Grain Seeds and Clothes

We never changed our minds.

But the way to the edge of the earth was too long,

And we never reached it.

Even if we spent our whole life on it,

We would never accomplish this mission.

So we had to give up

And started our journey home, disappointed.

Now we are nearly ninety-nine years of age,

Having spent all our life on the road.

We are fortunate to meet each other here today.

I advise you young fellows

To listen to me and change your mind.

The road ahead is long and full of evil,

Dangerous with tigers and wolves.

You should never follow our example

But return home at once.

Jiesu heard it and kept a long silence,

At last he had no choice

But to accept the old couple's advice.

He asked the old couple to go first,

And he and his companions would follow.

So the Emperor of Heaven and the queen

- 89 -

悄悄忙把天宫回。

再说姐苏领众人，
归心似箭日兼程。
两位老人没赶上，
途中又临一河畔。
忽见巨鸟体令噶，
凄然亡卧河边沙。
此鸟本非人间有，
人见不识心愕诧。
姐苏心细胆子大，
趋前左右仔细查。
只见三粒小果实，
静卧巨鸟羽翅下。
果实晶莹有光彩，
色绿明净又无瑕。
姐苏小心将果实，
仔细包裹藏筒帕①。
又将巨鸟来焚化，
然后率众急还家。

---

① 筒帕：德昂族等西南少数民族一种用手工织锦和刺绣工艺精心制作而成的随身挎包。

茶树、粮种和衣饰的来历
The Origin of Tea Trees, Grain Seeds and Clothes

Quietly went back to their heavenly palace.

Jiesu and his group
Hurried back without stopping.
They couldn't catch up with the old couple.
They were approaching another river
When he suddenly saw the huge bird Tilingga,
Lay sadly dead on the sand along the bank.
This bird had never been seen on the earth,
So everyone was astonished.
Jiesu was a careful and brave man.
He went closer to have a look.
He saw three little seeds
Beneath the huge bird's wings.
The seeds were bright and shining,
Green, clear and flawless.
Jiesu carefully wrapped them up,
And put them in his tongpa[①].
He then burned the great bird,
And rushed home with his companions.

---

① Tongpa: a shoulder bag carried by men of several ethnic groups in southwest China.

姐苏安然抵王宫，
妻儿聚首隔世同。
自忖所获果三粒，
世上无有太稀奇。
随即将之做妙礼，
岳父王前敬献与。
王亦不识此何物，
接过手中细研睹。
随后命人种地上，
悉心守候善养护。
不料此物方入土，
三日茁长成绿树。
五日已至人腰高，
绿叶飘香世上无。
人人见了皆称奇，
视为吉兆天佑护。
据说姐苏献宝时，
王伸左手来接住。
倘若当时双手接，
定生金色菩提树。
再说国王见此景，
啧啧称奇言天物。

茶树、粮种和衣饰的来历
The Origin of Tea Trees, Grain Seeds and Clothes

Jiesu returned safely to the palace.

It had been a long time since he left his wife and children.

He thought that the three seeds he had gained

Were unique in the world.

So he presented them as a precious gift

To his father-in-law, the king.

The king did not recognize them either

And examined them carefully.

Later he ordered his men to plant them in the ground

And to take good care of them.

To their surprise, once the seeds were buried in the soil,

They grew into trees with green leaves in three days.

Five days later the trees reached a man's waist,

And the green leaves gave off an unknown fragrance.

Everybody was amazed to see this.

They regarded it as a sign of good fortune.

It was said that when Jiesu presented the treasures,

The king reached out his left hand for them.

If he had reached out both hands for them,

They would have turned into golden bodhi trees.

When the king saw the trees,

He marveled and said they were miracles,

心想既是上天赐，

必为灵药除疾苦。

于是令人采其叶，

捣碎化汁献王母。

王母以汁拭双眼，

双目即刻光明现。

从此王母得看见，

王宫上下尽开颜。

"雅日①、雅日"人人讲，

王宫美事全传遍。

后来"雅日"就变成，

王宫绿树之名称。

亦即现在茶叶树，

德昂仰赖之食物。

今后凡我儿孙辈，

无论飘泊于何处。

混尚毕姐体令噶，

彼之恩德要记住。

---

① 雅日：德昂语，意为看见了光明，后来即成为茶水的代名词，今天的傣族也将茶水叫作"雅日"。

茶树、粮种和衣饰的来历
The Origin of Tea Trees, Grain Seeds and Clothes

Thinking that it was a gift from heaven

And must be magic medicine for diseases.

So he asked his men to pick some leaves

Made them into juice, and offered it to the queen.

The queen wiped her eyes with the juice,

And her eyes immediately could see things.

Since the queen's eyes regained sight,

The whole royal court was excited and happy.

Everyone was talking about "yari①",

And the good news spread far and wide.

Later the word "yari" became

The name of the royal green trees.

They were the precursors of the tea trees we grow today,

Which are what the De'ang people rely on today.

In the future, we, the De'ang people

May travel around the world.

But wherever we go, we must remember

The kindness of Hun Shangbijie, Tilingga.

---

① Yari: In the De'ang language, it first meant "seeing the light", and later it became synonymous with tea. Today, the Dai people also call tea "yari".

二

再说从前我德昂,

数数迁徙往八方。

那时各族和睦处,

我族自北迁往南。

那时中国有国王,

本是天神来下凡。

天堂人间常来往,

心怀慈悯好心肠。

他见人们食野果,

他见人间乏少粮。

便从天国取谷种,

树叶包裹返国邦。

故名此物为"毫法"①,

亦称"包谷"何须讲。

国王先让汉族种,

然后再传我德昂。

---

① 毫法:德昂族和傣族对玉米的称谓,意为天上来的粮食。

茶树、粮种和衣饰的来历
The Origin of Tea Trees, Grain Seeds and Clothes

II

In the old days, our De'ang ancestors

Migrated frequently in all directions.

In those days, all ethnic groups co-existed harmoniously.

Our ancestors migrated from north to south.

There was a king in ancient China,

Who was said to be a god from heaven.

He travelled between heaven and earth,

And he was kind and merciful.

He saw people eating wild fruit

Because they lacked food.

So he wrapped grain seeds in leaves in heaven

And brought them back to his kingdom.

Therefore, the name for this grain is "haofa"[①],

And it was also known as corn.

The king first gave it to the Han people to grow,

And then it was passed on to us, the De'ang people.

---

① Haofa: the De'ang and Dai name for corn; "Haofa" means "food from heaven".

故又称其为"甫却"①，

从此人间又添粮。

那时国泰民又安，

天下清宁无灾殃。

那时动物与人类，

相距遥远各一方。

人们白天种包谷，

向晚合家暖洋洋。

这时天神来递言：

帕惹不久生人间。

人们得闻喜讯后，

几度欢喜几度忧。

欢喜只为帕惹降，

因少妙供故言愁。

时有大富长者君，

阿腊塔谛是其名。

他育七子皆翘楚，

还有七女尽贤淑。

心灵手巧七女儿，

---

① 甫却：德昂语，德昂族对玉米的另一称谓，意为汉族栽种的粮食。

茶树、粮种和衣饰的来历
The Origin of Tea Trees, Grain Seeds and Clothes

So it had another name, "bengque①",

Which added a new type of food in the world.

At that time people lived a peaceful life,

And there were no catastrophes in the world.

In those days animals and humans lived

Far apart from each other.

People grew corn in the daytime

And enjoyed life at home in the evening.

Then a god from heaven came with a message:

Pare would soon be born in the world.

When people heard the good news,

They were both happy and worried.

They were happy because Pare would be born,

But worried because they had little food for sacrifice.

At that time there was a rich senior man,

Whose name was Ala Tadi.

He had seven outstanding sons

And seven virtuous daughters,

Who were so skilled that they could weave one hundred

---

① Bengque: another De'ang name for corn, which means "food grown by the Han Chinese".

日织排布①一百二。

长者教人编织术，

教会人们穿衣裤。

他闻帕惹要出世，

欢喜发心来建寺。

寺宇建成极庄严，

唯缺供品上妙食。

洞悉此情混西迦，

也想行善供帕惹。

于是变作凡夫面，

离开天宫到人间。

此时长者与众人，

因乏妙供正愁颜。

天帝来到寺宇前，

他向众人来进谏：

"父老莫急听我讲，

乡亲悉心听我言。

现在人皆食野味，

用供帕惹太寒微。

---

① 排布："排"是当地民间惯用的长度单位，成年人两臂展开的长度为一排。"排布"是长度为一排的布。

The Origin of Tea Trees, Grain Seeds and Clothes

And twenty pieces of arm-span cloth[①] in one day.

The senior man taught people to knit

And to make clothes.

He heard about the coming birth of Pare,

And was delighted to build a temple.

It looked magnificent and solemn.

The only thing missing was good food for sacrifice.

Hun Xijia The Emperor of Heaven learned about this

And also wanted to make an offering to Pare.

So he changed himself into a man

And came down to the earth.

Now the senior man and other people

Were worried about the lack of a decent sacrifice.

The Emperor of Heaven came to the temple

And suggested to the crowd,

"Folks, don't worry

And listen to me carefully.

Now everybody eats wild fruit,

Which is too humble to offer to Pare.

---

① Arm-span cloth: Arm-span is a unit of length commonly used by local people. The length of an adult man's stretched arms is about five feet long. Arm-span cloth is a piece of cloth with the length of an arm-span.

包谷为供虽然好,
可是单一数又少。
我知遥远动物国,
上妙食物比人多。
智勇之士应前去,
动物国将妙食取。
此去路遥多险阻,
有谁愿往我相助?"
长者七子闻此言,
自告奋勇愿往前。
天帝兴赞为示路,
又授咒语护身符。
随后天帝返天庭,
七子辞亲上险途。

趟过河川六百六,
翻过山岭九十九。
七子来到牛王国,
问询妙食有没有。
牛王闻言把头摇,
引彼去往虎国求。
降服恶魔六百六,

茶树、粮种和衣饰的来历
The Origin of Tea Trees, Grain Seeds and Clothes

Though corn is good as a sacrifice,

It lacks both variety and amount.

I know there is a remote kingdom of animals,

Where there's more good food than people need.

Brave and wise men should go

And get food from the kingdom of animals.

But it's a dangerous journey,

Whoever wants to go will get my help."

The seven sons of the senior man heard this,

And they all volunteered to go.

The Emperor of Heaven praised them, showed them the way,

And taught them some mantras to protect themselves.

Then he returned to heaven, while the seven sons

Said goodbye to their family and set off.

They crossed six hundred and sixty rivers,

And climbed over ninety-nine mountains.

The seven sons came to the kingdom of oxen,

And asked if there was any good food.

The king shook his head

And led them to the kingdom of tigers.

They defeated six hundred and sixty demons

越过鬼域九十九。
七子来到虎王国,
问询妙食有没有。
虎王闻言把手摇,
引彼去往兔国求。
兔王同样把头摇,
引彼去往龙国求。
龙王引彼求蛇王,
蛇王引彼求马王。
马王引彼求羊王,
羊王引彼求猴王。
猴王引彼求鸡王,
鸡王引彼求狗王。
狗王引彼求猪王,
猪王引彼求鼠王。
只见鼠王身形巨,
嘴红腹圆毛又长。
门牙大如竹笋叶,
任人一见胆就寒。
猪王见了忙上前,
细把七子来历讲。
鼠王听了开心花,

茶树、粮种和衣饰的来历

The Origin of Tea Trees, Grain Seeds and Clothes

And passed through ninety-nine ghost realms.

The seven sons came to the kingdom of tigers,

And asked if there was any good food.

The tiger king waved his hand

And led them to the kingdom of rabbits.

The rabbit king also shook his head

And led them to the kingdom of dragons.

The dragon king led them to the snake king,

Who led them to the horse king,

Who led them to the sheep king,

Who led them to the monkey king,

Who led them to the chicken king,

Who led them to the dog king,

Who led them to the pig king,

Who led them to the rat king.

The king of rats was very big.

He had a red mouth, round belly and long fur.

His front teeth was as big as the shells of bamboo shoots,

And anyone would be frightened at the sight of him.

The king of pigs approached him

And told him the story of the seven sons.

The king of rats heard the story and felt happy,

也要发心供帕惹。
连说妙食鼠国有，
不必再往他处求。
于是拿出食中魁，
名为谷子来相馈。
又令鼠国儿孙辈，
携食护送七子归。

七子归来众欢喜，
阿腊塔谛喜极泣。
随即请来动物客，
十二属类同庆贺。
七日七夜狂欢过，
谁也不回动物国。
从此人畜一域住，
直至如今和睦处。
因为感念动物恩，
十二属相配人人。
鼠因献食功劳大，
十二属中排老大。
阿腊塔谛长者公，
带领人们把谷种。

The Origin of Tea Trees, Grain Seeds and Clothes

Because he also wanted to offer a sacrifice to Pare.

He said that his kingdom had enough good food,

And the seven sons didn't have to go anywhere else.

Then he took out the best food,

Which was called rice.

He asked his sons and grandsons

To take some rice and escort the seven sons back.

The seven sons returned and the people felt thrilled,

And the senior Ala Tadi wept with joy.

Then the twelve animals were invited

To attend the celebration.

After seven days and seven nights of carnivals,

No one went back to the animal kingdoms.

From that time on, humans and animals have lived

In harmony in the same areas.

Because humans were grateful to the twelve animals,

Their names became the zodiac signs representing people.

As it was the rat that brought people rice,

It ranks first in the twelve-animal list.

The senior Ala Tadi

Led the people in planting rice.

收获粮食渐渐多,

从此不乏妙食供。

长者七子与七女,

又将衣服惠人众。

时有植物名曰"鲁①",

七女教人嚼又吐。

嚼后满口泛清凉,

人人喜爱成习俗。

从此人间衣食足,

唯待帕惹人间出。

那时人人都行善,

个个都将帕惹盼。

帕惹不久生人间,

人神鬼畜齐欢欣。

寺宇天天满人众,

妙食鲜花水果奉。

大家争相来顶礼,

帕惹尊前求皈依。

---

① 鲁:德昂语,系一种植物,德昂人取其叶,于内包裹石灰精、草烟、沙棘(德昂语,系一种植物名),然后放在嘴里反复咀嚼,和唾液混合后成红色,再吐出,德昂人称之为"嚼鲁子",据说长期这样做能保护牙齿。此习俗延续至今。

The Origin of Tea Trees, Grain Seeds and Clothes

They harvested more and more grain

And had good food for a decent sacrifice.

The seven sons and seven daughters of the senior man,

Shared their clothes with the people.

At that time there was a plant called betel①,

Which the seven daughters taught people to chew.

One's mouth felt cool after chewing it,

And everyone loved it and gradually it became a custom.

Since then, people had enough food and clothes,

And they were waiting for Pare to be born.

In those days everyone did good deeds

And waited for the arrival of Pare.

When Pare was born,

Gods, humans and animals rejoiced.

The temple was full of people every day,

Who came to offer food and fruits and flowers to Pare.

People rushed to the front of Pare

And pleaded to be blessed as Buddhists.

---

① Betel: It's a kind of plant and the De'ang people call it "lu". The De'ang people take its leaves to wrap lime extract, tobacco, and sea buckthorn. Then they chew the mixture repeatedly in their mouths. Mixed with saliva, they produce red juice, which is spit out again and again. The De'ang people call it "chewing luzi", which is said to have the function of protecting the teeth. This custom continues to this day.

时有谷神补唤毫①,

见此情形不服气。

变作一个丑乞丐,

要与帕惹比高低。

他强闯至帕惹前,

天神想拦拦不及。

人拜帕惹他不拜,

帕惹尊前傲然立。

帕惹问其欲何为,

答云欲与比高低。

众人闻言哄然笑,

笑此狂乞不量力。

三界②帕惹最为尊,

四生六趣③皆顶礼。

区区一个穷乞丐,

敢与帕惹比高低。

帕惹劝彼快回去,

---

① 补唤毫:德昂族和傣族对谷神(谷魂)的称谓,他主宰着粮食的丰盈和减损。
② 三界:佛经中说此世界众生所居之欲界、色界和无色界。欲界众生生活在男女饮食之欲当中,色界众生已经没有了男女饮食之欲,其生命唯有不同层次微妙的光色;无色界众生就连微妙的光色都超越了,他们生活于不同层次的空灵境界之中。
③ 四生六趣:佛经中将众生生命出生的型态分为胎生、卵生、湿生和化生四种类型,故称为四生;将众生生命的层次由低到高分为地狱、饿鬼、畜生、人、阿修罗、天六大种类,所以称为六趣,或称六道。

The Origin of Tea Trees, Grain Seeds and Clothes

At that time there lived a god of rice named Buhuanhao[①],

Who was unhappy to see this.

He changed himself into an ugly beggar

And wanted to challenge Pare.

He forced his way in front of Pare.

Even the gods from heaven couldn't stop him.

Everyone worshiped and bowed to Pare,

But he stood defiantly before Pare.

Pare asked him what he wanted to do,

And he said he wanted to compete with Pare.

The crowd laughed at him,

Saying the beggar was unreasonably arrogant.

Pare was the most revered in the Three Realms[②].

Even Four Lives and Six Species[③] respected him.

---

① Buhuanhao: the De'ang and Dai people's appellation for the god of rice, who controls the abundance or failure of grain.

② The Three Realms: It refers to the Desire Realm, the Material Realm, and the Nonexistence Realm of the living beings in this world, as mentioned in the Buddhist scriptures. In the Desire Realm, the sentient beings live with a desire for sex and food. In the Material Realm, the sentient beings have no desire for sex or food, and their lives have only different levels of subtle light. In the Nonexistence Realm, the sentient beings have no desire or even levels of subtle light; they live in different levels of ethereal state.

③ Four Lives and Six Species: In the Buddhist scriptures, the birth types of beings are divided into four types: viviparous, oviparous, wet, and metaplastic, and they are called Four Lives. According to the sins made and the consequences of the sins, the sentient beings are supposed to live in different worlds, therefore, the levels of sentient beings are divided into six categories: hell, hungry ghosts, beasts, humans, asura, and heaven, and this is called Six Species.

我高你低不用比。
见此情形补唤毫，
内心更加没好气。
答言既然比我高，
从此休将我寻觅。
言罢扭头往外走，
似云如烟悄然离。

再说帕惹至食时，
香妙斋饭味尽失。
方知来者为谷神，
要与帕惹比本事。
于是帕惹出了门，
急飞空中寻谷神。
帕惹看见补唤豪，
黑暗国里来藏身。
于是飞往黑暗国，
要把谷神亲手捉。
谷神一看势不妙，

茶树、粮种和衣饰的来历
The Origin of Tea Trees, Grain Seeds and Clothes

How could a poor beggar of no significance

Dare to compete with Pare?

Pare advised him to go back,

Saying that he was no match for him.

Hearing that,

Buhuanhao became even more angry.

He said that since Pare was more powerful,

Pare should not go and look for him.

With that, he turned and left

As quietly as a cloud.

When Pare had his meal,

He found the smell and taste of the food was gone.

He realized that the beggar was the god of rice,

Who wanted to compete with him.

So Pare left the temple in a hurry,

And flew into the air to look for the god of rice.

Pare saw that he was hiding

In the kingdom of darkness,

So he flew there

And tried to catch him.

The god of rice realized the danger

急往东方天边躲。
帕惹又往东边追，
谷神又匿南天陲。
如是八方相追逐，
你来我往满天飞。
追得谷神气吁吁，
追得谷神真疲惫。
无奈变作小米虫，
急急爬上草木丛。
爬过一株又一株，
爬过一蓬又一蓬。
可是帕惹神通大，
最终捉住小米虫。
帕惹将其置钵内，
斋饭方复原滋味。

话说谷神变米虫，
带来人间恩情重。
凡经爬过之草木，
变成世间杂粮种。
黄豆黑豆种种豆，
高粱麦子小米同。

茶树、粮种和衣饰的来历
The Origin of Tea Trees, Grain Seeds and Clothes

And rushed to the eastern horizon to hide himself.

Pare chased him further into the eastern horizon,

But the god of rice fled to the southern horizon.

Fleeing and chasing,

They two were busy flying in all directions in the air.

Pare's pursuit made the god of rice

Breathless and exhausted.

He had to change himself into a rice worm,

And crawl into the grass and bush.

He crawled past leaf after leaf

And bush after bush.

But Pare had great magic powers

And eventually caught the rice worm.

He put it in a bowl

And the smell and taste of the food returned.

In fact, the god of rice turning into the rice worm

Had made great contribution to the world.

All the grass and bushes he had crawled past

Turned into various kinds of grain for humans.

They were soya beans, black beans, and all other beans,

Sorghum, millet and wheat.

皆由此来莫忘记,
凡我儿孙记心中。
如果人类无粮食,
金银再多也没用。
百姓一天不能离,
王公离此也驾薨。
是故德昂诸儿女,
达古达楞语牢记。
定当尊敬于粮食,
颗颗粒粒要珍惜。

三

此时天地臻和祥,
人人心地怀善良。
世间坏人无一个,
百姓安乐幸福享。
此时人寿四万岁,
人类福寿似绵长。
此时帕惹出世间,

茶树、粮种和衣饰的来历
The Origin of Tea Trees, Grain Seeds and Clothes

All these were the gift of the god of rice,

And we should all remember this in our heart.

If humans don't have food to eat,

It is no use having much gold and silver.

Common people can't survive without rice,

And even the noble can't live without it.

So we De'ang people should all bear in mind

The story of Da-gu Da-leng.

We should all show respect for food

And treasure every single grain.

III

Now life was peaceful both in heaven and on the earth,

And everyone was kind-hearted.

No one in the world was mean,

And the people enjoyed happiness.

At that time a person could live forty thousand years,

A very long life indeed.

Also at that time, Pare was born into the world,

其名号曰果嘎散①。

此时德昂受彼教，

人人皈依行十善②。

此时我族最繁荣，

其中一支居永昌③。

于内有一阿拢④出，

空中来回常飞翔。

及至长成青年郎，

英俊潇洒美名扬。

一日阿拢戏空中，

不觉来到鸟王宫。

鸟王有女芳龄妙，

聪明美丽明月同。

阿拢一见难分舍，

不期缘遇情独钟。

---

① 果嘎散：据佛典《长阿含经》卷一载，贤劫中人寿四万岁时此佛出世。果嘎散为过去七佛之第四佛，贤劫千佛之第一佛，南传佛教五佛（即：过去佛"果嘎散、果腊贡、嘎撒巴、果达玛"和未来佛"阿力密地雅"）之第一佛。汉传佛教翻译为"拘留孙佛"，意为领持、灭累、所应断已断、成就美妙等。
② 十善：佛学名词，又名十善业道，为趣入佛道之基础，尤为在家居士所必修。十善分别是：身不造杀生、偷盗、邪淫，口不造妄言、绮语、两舌、恶口，意不造贪、嗔、痴。
③ 永昌：今保山市的古称。
④ 阿拢：德昂族和傣族民间对于传说中的英雄人物、智者及代表正义人物的尊称，佛祖释迦牟尼本生故事中诸多转世亦用此尊称。

茶树、粮种和衣饰的来历
The Origin of Tea Trees, Grain Seeds and Clothes

And he was named Guogasan①.

The De'ang people received education from him.

They were all converted to Buddhism and practiced the ten virtues②.

The De'ang people of that time were the most prosperous.

One De'ang branch lived in the Yongchang③ area.

They had a wise hero named Along④,

Who often flew back and forth in the air.

When he grew up into a young man,

He became even more handsome and well-known.

One day Along was flying for fun in the air

And came to the birds' palace by chance.

The king of birds had a young daughter,

---

① Guogasan: According to the first volume of the Buddhist scripture Chang-A-Han Sutra, Buddha Guogasan was born when a human being's life span was 40,000 years. Guogasan is the fourth of the seven Buddhas of the past phase, the first of the Thousand Buddhas of the present phase, and the first of the five Buddhas of Theravada Buddhism (i.e. four Past Buddhas: Guogasan, Guolagong, Gasaba, Guodama, and the Future Buddha, Alimidiya). Chinese Buddhism translates him as "Buddha Juliusun", which means to lead, to destroy, to be judged, and to achieve wonderful achievements.

② Ten virtues: It's a Buddhist term, also known as the ten good karma. It is the foundation needed to achieve Buddhahood with unremitting effort, and it is especially required for those Buddhists who worship at home. The ten virtues are: no killing, no stealing, no adultery, no false words, no sweet talk, no quarreling, no bad words, no desire, no anger, and no ignorance.

③ Yongchang: today's Baoshan City.

④ Along: It is a common name used by De'ang and Dai people for respectable legendary heroes, wise men and righteous people. This honorary title is also frequently used in many incarnations of Buddha Sakyamuni.

鸟之公主见阿拢，
亦自钟情芳心动。
从此俩人心相许，
月下海誓又山盟。
阿拢欲娶鸟王女，
鸟女要做阿拢妻。
于是来到鸟王前，
请求鸟王来同意。
鸟王也自心欢喜，
于是开口语其女：
"人类食熟鸟啖生，
生活习惯各相异。
儿若始终不后悔，
便做阿拢人间妻。"
公主答言决无悔，
阿拢亦言永相依。
于是二人结连理，
欢天喜地返人间。

茶树、粮种和衣饰的来历
The Origin of Tea Trees, Grain Seeds and Clothes

Who was smart and as beautiful as the moon.

Along saw the girl and couldn't tear himself away,

As he had fallen so deeply in love with her.

The bird princess also fell in love with Along

At first sight.

Since then the two hearts were dedicated to each other

And vowed to be together forever.

Along wished to marry the bird princess,

And the bird princess also wanted to be Along's wife.

Then they went to the king of birds

And requested permission from him.

The king was also pleased,

So he said to his daughter,

"Humans eat cooked food while birds eat raw food,

So you have different living habits.

If you think you won't regret it,

You can marry Along and be his wife."

The princess said she would never regret,

And Along promised he would love her forever.

So they got married

And merrily went back to earth.

嫁到人间鸟公主，
生活与人难相符。
人类食熟她啖生，
食罢余血沾胸脯。
故我后来德昂妇，
皆用红色饰胸部。
由于吃住不习惯，
鸟女频回娘家住。
隔三公主娘家回，
差五阿拢又接归。
如此往返有几多，
鸟王亦自看不过。
于是便从公主身，
拔下数羽编圈成。
王又诵咒向圈吹，
羽圈美丽又生辉。
然后将圈付女婿，
附耳再教阿拢计。
阿拢得计心欢喜，
携妻又返人间栖。
次日公主语阿拢，
要求一赏羽圈奇。

茶树、粮种和衣饰的来历
The Origin of Tea Trees, Grain Seeds and Clothes

The bird princess had married into the human world

And had a hard time adapting to the human way of life.

Humans ate cooked food while she ate raw food.

After the meal there was blood stain on her chest.

That's why the De'ang women

Decorate the bodice in red.

Because she was not accustomed to the new living habits,

The bird princess often went back to her parents' home.

Every few days she went there,

And every few days Along went to take her back.

This continued for a long time,

And the king of birds felt ashamed.

He picked a few feathers off of the princess

And knitted them into some wreathes.

The king blew some mantras to the wreathes,

Which suddenly glowed in a beautiful way.

He then gave them to his son-in-law,

And whispered a scheme to him.

Along was so glad

That he brought his bird wife back to earth.

The next day the bird princess

Requested to look at the feather wreathes.

阿拢便将羽圈示，
语妻此是鸟父礼。
公主一见爱喜极，
欲将羽圈佩娇躯。
阿拢不忍相阻劝，
奈何公主不听谏。
她将小圈套脚上，
又将中圈套脖间。
然后又在齐腰部，
套上五色最大圈。
妆罢临水将影照，
自觉美丽倍从前。
公主婀娜向阿拢，
娇问新妆美若何？
阿拢连声称好看，
赞彼美丽赛天仙。
公主听了心欢喜，
于是展翅欲飞天。
原本她想回鸟国，
新妆取怡父母前。
不料怎也飞不动，
情急便要除羽圈。

茶树、粮种和衣饰的来历
The Origin of Tea Trees, Grain Seeds and Clothes

Along showed them to her

And told her they were gifts from her father.

The princess loved them at first sight

And started to put them around her body.

Along tried to stop her,

But the princess didn't listen.

She put the small loops around her feet

And the medium ones around her neck.

Then around her waist,

She put on the largest and most colorful wreathes.

She looked at herself in the water,

And felt she was much more beautiful than before.

The princess seductively came to Along

And asked if her new ornaments were beautiful.

Along sang high praise of them

And said she was more beautiful than the fairies.

Hearing it the princess was so happy

That she spread her wings and tried to fly.

She wanted to fly back to the kingdom of birds

To show her parents her new ornaments.

To her surprise, she couldn't fly,

So she tried to remove the feather wreathes,

左脱右脱除不了,
阿拢力助也等闲。
方知鸟父施法术,
不让再回父身边。
从此公主不能飞,
只能永留在人间。

后来凡我德昂妇,
衣饰皆效公主服。
五颜六色集为美,
槟榔红嘴染齿黑。
头戴尖帽如鸟女,
身佩腰箍美又奇。
脚箍项圈为严饰,
奇异风俗代代传。

The Origin of Tea Trees, Grain Seeds and Clothes

But could not, no matter how hard she tried.

Along's help was also in vain.

Only then did she know that it was her father's

Trick to prevent her from returning home.

From then on the princess couldn't fly

And had to stay in the human world forever.

Ever since then when the De'ang women make clothes,

They follow the style of the princess' costume.

As dressing colorfully is considered beautiful, they chew betel nuts

To make their mouths red and their teeth black.

They wear pointed hats like a bird's head

And waistbands that are beautiful and exotic.

They also wear ankle hoops and necklaces as decorations,

And these special customs have been passed on from generation to generation.

太阳王子和龙公主

The Sun Prince and the Dragon Princess

那时四神布阿婆，
昼夜还没计算出。
年月四季尚未分，
冷热旱雨节度无。
雨则数年无晴天，
大地几尽成海湖。
晴则经年不见雨，
沃野万里变焦土。
唯有高山深洼里，
才生青草与果木。
人与动物赖此活，
供给稀少食口多。
人们只好八方去，
寻觅食物讨生活。
楚雄大理及永平，
临沧普洱与昌宁。
景洪勐海至勐腊，
丽江永昌到耿马。
思茅景东另双江，
布古勐广又阿瓦。

太阳王子和龙公主
The Sun Prince and the Dragon Princess

In the time before the four gods of fire, wind, water and earth

Had worked out a plan to divide day and night,

There was no division of years, months or seasons,

Nor was there a regulation of cold, hot, dry and rainy days.

Now there was rain for years without sunshine,

And the land almost became a sea,

Then there was sunshine for years without rain,

And the fertile fields became scorched earth.

Only in the high mountains and deep valleys

Could green grass and fruit trees grow.

People and animals lived on those,

But the supply was scarce and the population was large.

People had to move to other places

To find enough food to survive.

They moved to Chuxiong, Dali, Yongping,

Lincang, Pu'er, Changning,

Jinghong, Menghai, Mengla,

Lijiang, Yongchang, Gengma,

Simao, Jingdong, Shuangjiang,

Bugu, Mengguang and Awa.

达古达楞格莱标 // Da-gu Da-leng Gelaibiao

贤玉①嵊弄无数域，
皆是先祖曾居地。
哪有绿色芭蕉树，
哪有食物哪里居。
每至一处住山洞，
还有野兽来争栖。
人间那时太艰辛，
诸神上天去求情。
天帝依策布阿婆，
日月四季循律行。
如此大地渐渐苏
人间方始见荣兴。

达古达楞德昂祖，
漫长迁徙心酸路。
那时又至陌生地，
此地及村名称无。
但见三五领头人，
空中去来又飞舞。
便将此地称混敏②，

---

① 贤玉、勐广、阿瓦、布古：地名，皆位于今天的缅甸境内。贤玉与布古具体位置待考，勐广为今天缅甸的仰光，阿瓦为今天缅甸的瓦城。
② 混敏即勐混敏。

太阳王子和龙公主
The Sun Prince and the Dragon Princess

Xianyu[①] Lainong, were also places

The De'ang ancestors moved to and lived in.

Wherever there were green banana trees and food,

They settled there.

Wherever they moved, they lived in caves,

In which they had to compete for space with wild animals.

Life was so hard at that time

That the gods went to the Emperor of Heaven for help,

Who followed the advice of the four gods of mercy

To regulate the movement of the sun, the moon and the seasons.

So the earth came back to life,

And prosperity began to be seen in the human world.

Da-gu Da-leng, the De'ang ancestors,

Experienced a long and arduous migration.

Later they arrived at a strange place,

Which had no name.

There were several leaders,

Who flew back and forth in the air.

They called this place Hunmin[②],

[①] Xianyu, Mengguang, Awa, Bugu: All these are names of places located in today's Myanmar. The exact location of Xianyu and Bugu is not yet clear, but Mengguang is today's Yangon and Awa is today's Mandalay.

[②] Hunmin: It's also called Meng Hunmin. See note 1 on page 57.

于此长时得安住。

彼时混敏有大湖,
湖内住着龙公主。
公主年轻又美丽,
天仙亦难比肩出。
人间情状她久闻,
可是无由亲眼睹。
于是出水到岸边,
想将人间看清楚。
其时天帝混西迦,
敕命日月循律出。
人间四季初形成,
大地万物生机复。
太阳王子苏丽雅,
此时人间来巡察。
正好来到湖岸边,
巧遇公主芙蓉面。
他慕公主仪容美,
公主爱他英俊颜。
一朝相遇情有钟,
两厢倾诉海山盟。

太阳王子和龙公主
The Sun Prince and the Dragon Princess

And they lived there for quite a long time.

There used to be a great lake in Hunmin,

And in the lake lived the dragon princess,

Who was young and beautiful.

Even a fairy could hardly compare with her.

She had heard much about the human world,

But she had never had any chance to see it.

So she came out of the lake and reached the shore,

Wishing to have a good look at the human world.

At that time the Emperor of Heaven, Hun Xijia,

Ordered the sun and the moon to move regularly.

That was the time when seasons were formed,

And the earth was full of life.

Then the sun prince

Was sent to inspect the human world.

He happened to pass by the shore of the lake

And meet the beautiful princess.

He admired her beauty,

And she appreciated his handsome looks.

They fell in love at first sight,

And vowed to be true to each other.

及至临别尤依依,
彼此难舍难分离。
从此每隔一七日,
俩人岸边复相聚。
如此不觉时光移,
公主已然身有孕。
一天二人又相聚,
公主含情对郎语:
"眼看孩儿要出生,
哥哥何时将我娶?"
王子紧握公主手,
低声软语相抚慰:
"妹莫忧来妹莫愁,
哥我定要娶妹妹。
待我太阳宫里回,
将你我情禀父王。
然后再来娶妹归,
白头偕老长相偎。"
公主闻言心头暖,
依依送别暗拭泪。

王子回到太阳宫,

太阳王子和龙公主
The Sun Prince and the Dragon Princess

When they had to part,

It was hard to say goodbye.

Every six days

The two got together on the shore.

Time went by quickly,

And now the princess was pregnant.

One day they met again,

And the princess said to her love,

"The baby will soon be born,

But when will you marry me?"

The prince grasped the princess' hand,

And told her with soothing words,

"Don't worry.

I'm going to marry you soon.

After I return to the sun palace,

I will tell my father about our love.

Then I will come back and marry you,

And we will stay together forever."

The princess' heart was warmed up by these words.

Wiping away her tears, she saw the prince off.

When the prince returned to the sun palace,

禀父欲娶龙女回。
阳父闻说赤颜暗,
斥子痴迷情网坠:
"太阳国度烈焰熊,
龙宫殿里寒溟水。
儿往龙宫不禁寒,
她住阳城烈焰摧。
冷热本是天生克,
岂能相容来和合。
儿若执意娶龙女,
父决不许万难可。"
太阳王子闻父言,
据理再将父王劝:
"冷热虽然难调和,
阳城龙宫非所宜。
然而人间冷暖适,
我与龙女可居栖。
儿恳父王允我求,
人间两情结连理。
父王若能遂儿请,
天宫富贵儿甘弃。"
阳父闻听赤颜怒,

太阳王子和龙公主
The Sun Prince and the Dragon Princess

He told his father that he wanted to marry the dragon princess.

The sun king was angry.

He scolded his son for his obsession with love:

"The kingdom of the sun is a burning place,

While the dragon palace is filled with icy-cold water.

You cannot bear the cold if you live in the dragon palace,

And she cannot stand the heat if she lives in the sun city.

Heat and cold are destined to be opposed to each other,

How can they be mixed and blended?

If you insist on marrying the dragon daughter,

You will not have my permission."

Hearing what his father said,

The sun prince pleaded once again,

"Heat and cold are difficult to reconcile,

And neither of the two palaces are suitable for the two of us,

But the human world is good,

And I will live there with the dragon princess.

I beg and hope that Your Majesty will permit us

To marry in the human world.

If Your Majesty kindly grants my request,

I will give up my wealth and rank in heaven."

His father was outraged.

厉声斥子太糊涂。
何得放弃天宫贵,
甘做人间一凡庶。
阳父敕命将王子,
太阳宫里来禁锢。
何时他悔心意转,
何时将他来放出。

王子幽禁在阳宫,
心思只在龙宫中。
日也思来夜也想,
担心公主孕身重。
奈何此身陷囹圄,
想往探视梦却空。
掐指一算产期近,
自却幽闭在深宫。
忧念公主心如焚,
叫天不应声声恸。
此时王子倍担忧,
湖畔公主相思痛。
何法解得情人愁,
辗转反侧一计穷。

太阳王子和龙公主
The Sun Prince and the Dragon Princess

He scolded his son for being so foolish,

Willing to give up everything in heaven

To be a commoner in the human world.

The sun king ordered the sun prince

To be imprisoned in the palace.

Only when the son showed his regret

Would he be released.

The prince was shut up in the sun palace,

But his mind was on the dragon palace.

Day and night,

He worried about the pregnant princess,

But, as he was helplessly imprisoned,

He could not go and see her.

He knew the baby was soon to be born,

But he was still shut up deep in the palace.

Sorrow burned the prince's heart,

But no one would come to help him.

He was worried

That the princess would be love-sick.

He was racking his brain

For what to do, but in vain.

偶然回首窗前看，
金色乌鸦来相望。
王子此时灵机动，
面对金乌开口讲：
"金乌金乌听我言，
你本仙鸟我收养，
往日待你不薄情，
从来最听我号令。
如今我身失自由，
尚有要事你分忧。
我有随身一筒帕，
内装宝瓶号如意。
宝瓶能满诸需求，
公主所需应尽有。
你今替我往人间，
筒帕亲交公主手。
公主乃我心上人，
分娩在即我担忧。
你要代我将公主，
好言慰抚莫忧愁。"

金乌听罢王子言，

太阳王子和龙公主
The Sun Prince and the Dragon Princess

By chance, he looked at the window and found

That his golden crow came to see him.

The prince hit upon an idea

And said to the golden crow,

"Golden crow, please listen to me.

You are an immortal bird raised by me.

I have treated you kindly,

And you have always obeyed me.

Now I have lost my freedom

And need your help.

I have a tongpa,

In which I put a precious bottle named "As You Wish".

As the bottle can satisfy every need,

It is what the princess needs now.

Please go down to earth for me

And give the tongpa to the princess in person.

The princess is my sweetheart.

I'm worried because she is to have my baby soon.

Go and visit the princess for me,

And tell her not to worry."

The golden crow obeyed the prince

即刻领命下九天。
口衔筒帕展羽翅，
不久来到人世间。
人间山水美如画，
金乌赏忘倍流连。
它见山林多果木，
种种水果大又甜。
不禁满心生欢喜，
忙将筒帕挂路边。
且将鲜果一一尝，
越尝越美入林间。
路边树梢筒帕挂，
早就忘却九云天。
此时恰逢一路客，
树梢筒帕乍看见。
好奇取下往里看，
如意宝瓶光耀眼。
路人见此贪心起，
四顾无人遂据取。
然后取来牛马粪，
置入筒帕复挂回。
再说金乌食足饱，

太阳王子和龙公主
The Sun Prince and the Dragon Princess

And immediately flew down to earth.

With the tongpa in its mouth,

It soon reached the human world.

The world was a picturesque landscape,

And the golden crow indulged itself in it.

It saw fruit on the trees in the mountains,

And all the fruits were big and sweet.

Filled with joy,

It hung the tongpa on a tree by the path

And started to taste the fresh fruits.

The more he ate, the further into the woods he went,

Forgetting all about the tongpa

It hung on the tree.

There happened to be a passerby,

Who saw the tongpa hanging on the tree.

Curiously he took the tongpa down and looked into it,

And saw the bottle shining brilliantly.

The greedy passerby saw no one nearby

And stole the bottle.

Then he fetched some dung,

And put them in the tongpa and put it back.

When the golden crow had had plenty of food,

归见筒帕挂原位。
随即取下至湖畔，
交予公主道原委。
又将王子慰抚语，
转述公主天宫回。
公主得信心稍慰，
遂将筒帕密收藏。

不久公主即临产，
生下五个金色蛋。
公主将蛋轻摸抚，
千头万绪绕心肠。
日思夜想心上人，
常自梦醒空惆怅。
此时公主忽想到，
王子相赠如意宝。
于是取出筒帕来，
睹物以息相思闹。
不料筒帕才打开，
牛粪马粪入眼来。
公主一看生了气，
牛粪马粪抛一地：

The Sun Prince and the Dragon Princess

It returned and saw the tongpa hanging in the same place.

It took down the tongpa, went to the lake,

Handed it to the princess and told her what had happened.

It then conveyed the prince's consolation to the princess

And returned to heaven.

The princess felt a bit relieved at the message

And put the tongpa away in a secret place.

Soon the princess was in labor.

She laid five golden eggs.

She fondled the eggs

And pondered her complicated situation.

Day after day and night after night she missed her love,

Often waking up sadly from a dream.

Then suddenly the princess remembered

The bottle that the prince had given her.

She took out the tongpa

And thought of the prince.

But when the tongpa was opened,

Animal dung caught her eye.

The princess was very angry.

She threw the dung all over the ground.

"王子你呀负心郎,
怎可无情将我欺。
我在人间受诸苦,
桩桩件件皆为你。
远离父母人间居,
十月怀孕不容易。
因你一诺我尽尝,
相思之苦难诉泣。
海誓山盟脑后抛,
背信负心把我弃。
如今又派金乌来,
编排好言将我戏。
既言送我如意宝,
何以畜粪将我欺!"
龙女仰天泪长流,
心里越想越生气。
她将五蛋轻抚摸,
凄凄楚楚伤心语:
"儿啊儿啊苦命儿,
尚未出世遭爹弃。
你们本是太阳子,
如今天宫不能去。

太阳王子和龙公主
The Sun Prince and the Dragon Princess

"Oh, Prince! You broke your vow!

How can you cheat me like this?

I have suffered a lot on earth,

And I have suffered it for you.

Here I am, away from my parents,

Going through the pain of pregnancy.

Because of your promise,

I have tasted the bitterness of yearning for you.

You have forgotten our vows,

And turned me away through treachery.

You made me a fool

By sending me the golden crow.

You said the gift was a lucky bottle,

But why did you deceive me with animal dung!"

The dragon princess looked up to heaven in tears.

The more she thought about it, the angrier she became.

She fondled the eggs,

And said sadly,

"My poor children,

You have been abandoned by your father before your birth.

You are the sons of the sun,

But the heavenly palace is not a place for you.

娘欲你等龙宫回，
龙宫水寒岂能居。
儿啊休怪娘无情，
缘儿只能人间栖。
娘今生儿无能育，
岂是娘亲将儿弃。
我既一错不再错，
儿等随缘人间寄。"
言罢将蛋抛空中，
返身入水下龙宫。

传说五个金色蛋，
各各落在不同方。
贤玉阿瓦与崃弄，
还有布古及勐广。
他们皆被德昂人，
拾回家中好安放。
日久五蛋一一裂，
出生五人好儿郎。
兄弟各自于五地，
繁衍生息代绵长。
按照出生先后序，

The Sun Prince and the Dragon Princess

Mother wants you to come to the dragon palace,

But how can you bear the icy-cold water there?

Oh my sons, will you not blame me as a merciless mother,

Because you can only live on earth?

Mother has given you life but cannot raise you,

So it's not true that I am abandoning you.

I have made one mistake and will not make another.

I'll leave you here to your fate."

Saying this, she threw the eggs into the air

And returned to the dragon palace underwater.

Legend has it that the five golden eggs

Fell to five different places:

Xianyu, Awa, Lainong,

Bugu, and Mengguang.

They were all brought home by the De'ang people,

And taken good care of.

Some time had passed and the five eggs

Hatched out five sons.

The five brothers lived in five different places

And produced many generations.

By birth order,

达古达楞话语传：

"贤玉为大最先出，

勐广次之阿瓦三。

四为布古五崃弄，

长幼有序要遵从。"

故我德昂原本是，

龙与太阳之传人。

无论辗转到何方，

承前启后本勿忘。

太阳王子和龙公主
The Sun Prince and the Dragon Princess

The De'ang legend Da-gu Da-leng recorded the story:

"The one born in Xianyu was the eldest brother.

The second, the third, the fourth, and the fifth

Were born in Mengguang, Awa,

Bugu and Lainong, respectively.

That is the birth order of the five brothers."

So we De'ang people were originally

The descendants of the dragon and the sun.

Wherever we roam, we should not forget our origins.

王宫斩龙
Killing the Dragon in the Royal Palace

达古达楞格莱标 // Da-gu Da-leng Gelaibiao

达古达楞代代传，

德昂历史说不完。

先有帕惹果嘎散，

出世教化国泰安。

果腊贡①与嘎撒巴②，

末后一位果达玛③。

四位帕惹先后出，

教会世人持善法。

那时中国有国王，

本是神仙来下凡。

那时我族居混敏，

信佛奉教心意专。

---

① 果腊贡：据佛典《长阿含经》卷一载，贤劫中人寿三万岁时此佛出生于清净城。果腊贡为过去七佛之第五佛，贤劫千佛之第二佛。南传佛教五佛之第二佛。汉传佛教翻译为"拘那含牟尼佛"，意为金色仙、金儒、金寂等。
② 嘎撒巴：据佛典《长阿含经》卷一载，贤劫中人寿二万岁时此佛出世。嘎撒巴为过去七佛之第六佛，贤劫千佛之第三佛，南传佛教五佛之第三佛。汉传佛教翻译为"迦叶佛"，意为饮光，乃是释迦牟尼佛前世之师。
③ 果达玛：释迦牟尼佛。释迦牟尼乃过去七佛之第七佛，贤劫千佛之第四佛，南传佛教五佛之第四佛，意为能仁。两千五百多年以前出生于古印度迦毗罗卫国（今尼泊尔境内），为国王净饭王的太子。释迦牟尼从小就聪明绝伦，十多岁时就通达了世间的各种学问，由于对生老病死等人生的根本问题产生困惑，于二十岁时悄然离家，遍访名师。后入雪山，经过六年苦行后，来到了尼连禅河畔的菩提树下入于禅定，于第七天深夜睹明星而觉悟宇宙人生的大道，成就佛果，这一年他三十二岁。成佛后，他遍游古印度各地传授佛法，开创佛教。四十九年后，于拘尸那迦城婆罗双树林入般涅槃（逝世）。

王宫斩龙
Killing the Dragon in the Royal Palace

Da-gu Da-leng has been passed on for generations.

The history of the De'ang people really has no end.

Guogasan was the first Pare

Who enlightened the De'ang people.

Following him were Guolagong① and Gasaba②,

---

① Guolagong: According to the first volume of the Buddhist scripture Chang-A-Han Sutra, Buddha Guolagong was born in Qingjing City when human life span was thirty thousand years. Guolagong is the fifth of the seven Buddhas in the Past Phase, the second of the Thousand Buddhas in the Present Phase and the second of the five Buddhas in Theravada Buddhism. Chinese Buddhism translates his name as "Buddha Junahanmouni", which means golden immortal.

② Gasaba: According to the first volume of the Buddhist scripture Chang-A-Han Sutra, Buddha Gasaba was born when human life span was twenty thousand years. Gasaba is the sixth of the seven Buddhas in the Past Phase, the third of the Thousand Buddhas in the Present Phase and the third of the five Buddhas in Theravada Buddhism. Chinese Buddhism translates his name as "Buddha Jiaye", which means "absorbing light". He is the teacher of Buddha Shakyamuni in his previous life.

时至今日德昂子,

供佛物品来历知。

南玉提洼① 鲜花奉,

伙喊曼沓供扎董②。

昆排③ 献上妙好香,

南朗④ 又将米花供。

宝银阿拢⑤ 燃蜡烛,

供养袈裟混尚弄⑥。

德昂先祖效前贤,

供佛传统代代奉。

那时德昂俱德智,

民风淳朴衣食丰。

---

① 南玉提洼:据德昂族民间传说,南玉提洼是一个长得很丑的女人,为了来世自己能够获得美丽的容颜,她采来各种美丽的鲜花供养佛陀。于是,她成为第一个用鲜花供佛的人。
② 伙喊曼沓供扎董:据德昂族民间传说,伙喊曼沓是德昂族古时候一个小部落的首领,是他最先用"扎"和"董"供佛的。"扎"和"董"是德昂族用纸剪出来的一种赕佛品,长度二十公分左右不等。"扎"就像一面长三角形的小彩旗。"董"则是圆头燕尾、外形似鱼的一种长条形剪纸。
③ 昆排:据德昂族民间传说,昆排是住在森林里的一种魔王,他最先将森林里的香木供养佛陀。
④ 南朗:据德昂族民间传说,南朗是个长得很黑的女人,为了求得来世相貌生得白皙美丽,她便用净白如雪的米花供佛。于是,她成为第一个用米花供佛的人。
⑤ 宝银阿拢:据德昂族民间传说,他是第一个燃蜡烛供佛的智勇之士。
⑥ 供养袈裟混尚弄:据德昂族民间传说,此世三灾过后,雷神劈开金色的大葫芦时,将天帝置于葫芦之上的金色袈裟存放于混尚弄(大天神)处,待佛出世的时候由混尚弄供献与佛。

王宫斩龙
Killing the Dragon in the Royal Palace

And the last one was Guodama① (Sakyamuni),

The four Pares were born one after another.

They taught people to be good and kind.

There was a king in China,

Who was a god from heaven.

At that time our De'ang ancestors lived in Hunmin.

They believed in Buddhism and worshiped Pare.

To this day De'ang descendants still know

The original history of the objects offered to Pare.

Nanyutiwa② was the first to offer flowers,

---

① Guodama: He is Buddha Shakyamuni. He is the seventh of the seven Buddhas in the Past Phase, the fourth of the Thousand Buddhas in the Present Phase and the fourth of the five Buddhas in Theravada Buddhism. Born more than 2,500 years ago in the ancient Indian Kingdom of Kapilavastu (now in Nepal), he was the prince of King Suddhodana. Shakyamuni was very clever from an early age. He learned all kinds of knowledge in the world when he was a teenager. Because he was confused about the fundamental issues of life, such as birth, aging, illness and death, he quietly left home at the age of 20 and visited famous teachers. Later, he entered the Snow Mountain. After six years of ascetic practice, he came to practice meditation under the linden tree along the Nairanjana River. On the seventh day, in the middle of the night, he saw the stars and realized the true meaning of life. After becoming Buddha, he traveled through ancient India. He taught people and spread Dharma wherever he went and Buddhism was thus created. Forty-nine years later, he died and entered the realm of nirvana rebirth in a wood in Kushinagar City.

② Nanyutiwa: According to De'ang folklore, Nanyutiwa was an ugly woman. In order to obtain a beautiful face in the next cycle of life, she collected various beautiful flowers to offer to Buddha. So she was considered the first person to use flowers as a sacrifice to Buddha.

达古达楞格莱标 // Da-gu Da-leng Gelaibiao

尔时混敏国王妻,
美貌绝伦无人比。
她在嫁与国王前,
倾倒无数骄子弟。
海中龙子曾同彼,
暗通情愫难分离。
及至嫁与国王后,
心犹念念龙子意。

王宫斩龙
Killing the Dragon in the Royal Palace

Huohanmanta was the first to offer cut papers,[1]

Kunpai[2] was the first to offer joss sticks,

Nanlang[3] was the first to sacrifice popped rice,

Baoyin'along[4] was the first to burn candles as a sacrifice,

And Hunshangnong[5] was the first to offer a kasāya to Pare.

The De'ang ancestors followed those great people of virtue

And passed on the tradition of sacrificing to Pare.

In those days, the De'ang people were wise, virtuous,

Simple and had enough food and clothing.

In those days, the queen of the Hunmin kingdom

Was beautiful beyond comparison.

Before she married the king,

---

[1] Huohanmanta; cut papers: According to De'ang folklore, Huohanmanta was the chief of a small De'ang tribe in ancient times. He was the first person to offer as a sacrifice materials cut out of paper, about 20 cm in length. The cut papers are like small buntings with long triangles or round-shaped dovetails with round heads and fish-like bodies.

[2] Kunpai: According to De'ang folklore, Kunpai was a demon living in the forest. He first provided Buddha with fragrant trees in the forest.

[3] Nanlang: According to De'ang folklore, Nanlang was a very dark-skinned woman. In order to obtain a fair and beautiful appearance in the next cycle of life, she used white, snow-like rice flowers to sacrifice to Buddha. As a result, she became the first person to use rice flowers to worship Buddha.

[4] Baoyin'along: According to De'ang folklore, he was the first wise man to burn candles for Buddha.

[5] Hunshangnong: According to De'ang folklore, after the three catastrophes in this world, when the thunder god split the golden gourd, the golden kasāya placed on the gourd by the Emperor of Heaven was stored at the major god Hunshangnong's place, to be offered to Buddha once he was born.

达古达楞格莱标 // Da-gu Da-leng Gelaibiao

一日龙子使神通,
偷偷潜入王宫中。
他与王后私相会,
云雨缠绵情迷醉。
为能两情长相守,
将害国王设阴谋。
及至夜深人又静,
乘着国王入梦顷。
事先潜藏龙公子,
现形利齿咬王死。
国王死因无人知,
朝政荒疏国待治。
于是大臣共聚商,
推举一位新国王。
不料新王不久长,
一夜之间又暴亡。

王宫斩龙
Killing the Dragon in the Royal Palace

She had so many famous suitors.

The dragon son in the sea

Was deep in love with her.

Even after she married the king,

She still cherished the affections of the dragon son.

One day the dragon son used his magic

And sneaked into the palace.

He met the queen secretly,

And they reveled in love-making.

In order to live together,

They worked out a plot to murder the king.

Late at night, when all was quiet,

The king had fallen in a sound sleep.

The hidden dragon son came out

And killed the king with his sharp teeth.

The cause of the king's death was unknown,

And the kingdom was out of joint.

So the ministers got together

And chose a new king.

But curiously the new king died

On the same night he was chosen to be king.

诸位大臣又重商,
再立一位新国王。
新王执政一月余,
一夕过后又死去。
国内三王接连死,
宫墙内外声声泣。
众位大臣又商议,
欲选国王再拥立。
可是朝野人惶惶,
谁人还敢做国王?

时有阿拢众所钦,
年方十七义勇名。
恶龙恶妇兴殃害,
他将此事看得明。
为保社稷国与家,
阿拢自荐做国君。
诸位大臣正着急,
国之王位无人继。
忽闻阿拢毛遂荐,
急忙聚首再商议。
最后一致齐推举,

王宫斩龙
Killing the Dragon in the Royal Palace

The ministers got together again,

And another new king was chosen.

He ruled the kingdom for more than one month

And was found dead early one morning.

Three kings had died one after another,

Sorrow and weeping were heard inside and outside of the palace.

The ministers met again

To choose a new king.

But both the court and the common people were terrified.

Who would dare to be king?

At that time there was a much-admired man named Along,

Who at seventeen was known for his courage and righteousness.

He saw it very clearly

That the evil dragon and the bad woman had caused the tragedies.

To protect the kingdom and the homeland,

Along recommended himself to be king of the kingdom,

All the ministers were anxious

That no one would ascend to the throne.

When they heard Along recommend himself,

They got together at once for a discussion.

They finally agreed and announced

国之王位阿拢继。

阿拢登基为国王,
入主王宫第一晚。
放言要与王后寝,
遂将王妻秘密禁。
密令找来半湿皮,
裹成人形似已眠。
然后手握三尺剑,
藏于床后房柱边。
其时房之柱心中,
早被恶龙咬一空。
及至夜深人静时,
万籁寂静人不知。
龙子便由房柱内,
悄悄潜出向床窥。
他见床上有人卧,
以为新王定无疑。
于是猛然扑上前,
死死咬住半湿皮。
不料龙牙被黏住,
情急欲拔不能出。

王宫斩龙
Killing the Dragon in the Royal Palace

That Along would inherit the throne of the kingdom.

The first night after Along became the king,

He declared that he would sleep with the queen.

He imprisoned the queen in a secret place.

Then he gave a secret order to find him a wet skin

And roll it into a human figure

Looking as if he was sleeping.

Holding a long sword in his hand,

He hid himself behind the pillar near the bed.

The heart of the pillar in the room

Had been bitten hollow by the dragon.

At midnight, when all was quiet

And silence reigned everywhere,

The dragon sneakily climbed out of the pillar

And peeked at the bed.

He saw someone lying in bed,

And thought it was the new king.

So he pounced upon the figure

And bit hard into the half-wet skin.

But the dragon's teeth were stuck in the skin,

And he couldn't pull them out.

阿拢趁机自床后，
挥剑斩断恶龙首。
龙子恶贯终满盈，
一命呜呼快人心。
阿拢又将奸淫妇，
王后恶行昭众臣。
然后命于第二日，
将其极刑来处死。
不料王后之腹内，
已孕无数小龙子。
如若小龙得出世，
必成殃害祸人间。
其时王后已被诛，
无数小龙自腹出。
阿拢急挥三尺剑，
将小恶龙一一除。
由于小龙实在多，
仍有两条被逃脱。
它们就是现在的，
绿色红尾剧毒蛇。

因此自从那时起，

王宫斩龙
Killing the Dragon in the Royal Palace

Along quickly rushed out from behind the pillar,

Wielded the sword and cut off the dragon's head.

The dragon's crimes were not able to be atoned for,

And his death brought great joy to the people.

Then Along made the queen's wickedness

Known to all his subjects

And gave the order that on the next day

The queen would be executed.

But in the queen's womb,

There were numerous baby dragons.

If the baby dragons were born,

They would harm people.

When the queen was killed,

Many little dragons came out of the womb.

Along quickly wielded his long sword

And killed the little dragons.

Because there were so many of them,

Two escaped.

They are now known

As the red-tailed green tree-viper.

After that,

德昂建房风俗移。
为防小龙从柱心，
潜入屋中兴殃害。
建房之时房中柱，
不能与地相接触。
立柱之前需先用，
红铁泡水浇中柱。
据说若遇小龙来，
柱似热铁缠不住。
如此小龙就不能，
缘柱上天兴荼毒。
立柱之时需先将，
房之中柱分两部。
一段立在楼房下，
另外一段房中竖。
如此小龙就不能，
咬空柱心房中入。
自从阿拢做国王，
风调雨顺人安住。
因此德昂立房柱，
代代相传缘此故。

Killing the Dragon in the Royal Palace

The De'ang people changed their house style.

To prevent the little dragons from

Getting out of the pillar to harm people,

When a new house was built,

The central pillars were raised above the ground.

Before the pillars were set up,

Water boiled with a hot iron was splashed on the pillars.

In this way, it is said,

If a little dragon should come,

The pillars would be too hot for it to slither up

And do harm to people.

When setting up a pillar,

The central pillars of the house

Were divided into two sections.

One section was located below the floor,

And the other stood above the floor.

In this way, the little dragon wouldn't

Be able to make the pillar hollow and sneak into the room.

From the time Along became king of the kingdom,

Everything went smoothly and people lived in harmony.

This is how the De'ang people's way of setting up pillars

Has been passed on from generation to generation.

漫漫坎坷迁徙路
A Long and Arduous Journey of Migration

达古达楞格莱标 // Da-gu Da-leng Gelaibiao

一

时果达玛已入灭①,
人失明灯多灾劫。
天帝忧人少敬信,
将佛经典藏天界。
从此德昂多信鬼,
内外处处鬼神供。
持善法者日渐少,
人心变换多恶劣。
长上无慈无所惧,
下无敬信常行邪。
孝悌忠信全不顾,
父子儿女五伦缺。
那时德昂势力强,
他族面前骄气扬。
若见汉傣小商贩,
即行恶作坏水酿。
若遇傣姥坐竹筏,
行蛮将其赶水下。

---

① 入灭：佛典用语，意为逝世、死亡。

漫漫坎坷迁徙路
A Long and Arduous Journey of Migration

I

When Guodama had entered the realm of nirvana[①],

Humans lost his guidance and suffered from disasters.

The Emperor of Heaven worried about man's lack of faith,

So he enshrined the Buddhist scriptures in heaven.

From that time, most De'ang people believed in ghosts

And offered sacrifices to ghosts everywhere.

There were fewer and fewer believers in Buddhism,

And people's morality degenerated.

The elders showed no mercy and feared nothing,

While the young were not respectful and did evil deeds.

No one cared about filial piety and loyalty,

And traditional family ethics were not followed.

At that time, the De'ang people were powerful,

So they were arrogant toward other people.

When they saw Han or Dai peddlers,

They did wicked things to them.

When they saw an old Dai woman on a bamboo raft,

They brutally drove her into the river.

---

① Enter the realm of nirvana: It's a Buddhist term, meaning "to die" or "pass away".

若见小脚汉族女,
强将裹脚解又拉。
令其赤脚而走履,
才被火烧茅草地。
逢集上街向傣族,
买物专讲德昂语。
虽言买物却时常,
机巧跋扈钱不与。
忍无可忍傣族怒,
最先兴兵行报复。
无奈众寡太悬殊,
交战不久即败溃。
傣族愈恨心不甘,
将众援军四处搬。
卷土重来复与战,
一鼓作气克城关。
勐腊勐海与景洪,
思茅景东又双江。
德昂无奈且退至,
澜沧耿马及永昌。
此役双方伤亡重,
数载休战暂相安。

漫漫坎坷迁徙路
A Long and Arduous Journey of Migration

When they saw a Han woman with small feet,

They forced her to unbind the cloth wrapping her feet

And made her walk barefooted

On the cogon grass that had just been burned.

When they bought objects from Dai traders in the market,

They spoke the De'ang language to them.

Though they said they would buy things,

More often than not they didn't pay for them.

Finally, the Dai people could not bear it

And waged a war to retaliate.

But they were outnumbered

And overwhelmed.

As a result, they hated the De'ang people even more.

They found reinforcements from other tribes.

They staged a comeback

And defeated these De'ang territories in one stroke:

Mengla, Menghai, Jinghong,

Simao, Jingdong and Shuangjiang.

The De'ang people had no choice but to retreat

To Lancang, Gengma and Yongchang.

There were heavy casualties on both sides,

And a temporary peace was secured for some years.

达古达楞格莱标 // Da-gu Da-leng Gelaibiao

可是我族恶难除，

处处惹事又生非。

终于傣族又发怒，

再次兴兵伐我族。

那时德昂尚强大，

数次攻打而不下。

傣族无奈遣使节，

联络汉族共相伐。

那时汉族亦早已，

不满德昂太蛮霸。

于是傣汉共举兵，

联军首先犯昆明①。

那时昆明德昂据，

数名勇士会飞行。

他们自恃俱勇武，

己方人多势力足。

飞行空中放狂言，

要将傣汉尽铲除。

岂料联军攻势猛，

---

① 昆明：具体地点是否是指现在的昆明，和前述"混敏"是否异同，诵者也不能说清楚，尚待考证。

A Long and Arduous Journey of Migration

But our people's wickedness was hard to get rid of.

They made trouble here and there.

At last the Dai people got annoyed again

And launched another attack on the De'ang people.

At that time, the De'ang people were still strong,

So they survived several battles.

The Dai had no choice but to send their envoys

To unite with the Han to fight the De'ang people.

The Han people at that time

Were already dissatisfied with the De'ang people.

An allied Dai and Han army

Attacked Kunming[①] first.

Kunming was inhabited by De'ang people,

And several De'ang warriors could fly.

They were confident in their own valor

And great number and power.

Flying in the air, they shouted that

They would uproot all the Dai and Han people.

But the allied forces were on the offensive.

---

① Kunming: Whether the specific location refers to the current Kunming and whether it is similar to or different from the aforementioned place "Meng Hunmin", the storyteller was not sure. This remains yet to be verified.

又向勇士施法术。
德昂勇士遂落地,
身疲瑟瑟不能敌。
联军趁机陷城池,
尽将德昂戮无余。
待到勇士体力复,
只好逃飞永昌府。
联军随后克大理,
德昂首尾难相顾。
无奈只好死守住,
楚雄昌宁等城阜。

如此相持经数载,
烽烟又起殃祸来。
最先傣汉兵与民,
常常无故失踪影。
联军认是德昂为,
又兴大军动刀兵。
敌兵遍野多如蜂,
傣汉军似雨天云。
数次交战皆溃败,
村庄尽被敌兵占。

漫漫坎坷迁徙路
A Long and Arduous Journey of Migration

They cast spells on the De'ang warriors,

Who lost their flying power and dropped to the ground,

Exhausted and unable to fight.

The allies seized the opportunity

To conquer the De'ang city, killing all inside.

When the warriors regained their strength,

They had to flee to Yongchang prefecture.

The allied forces then went on to conquer Dali,

And the De'ang people had nowhere to go.

They had to go all out

To defend Chuxiong, Changning and other cities.

Peace had been going on for years,

But one day another war started.

At first some Dai and Han soldiers and people

Were inexplicably missing.

Assuming that the De'ang people were to blame,

The allied forces attacked the De'ang people again.

The enemy soldiers were everywhere, like bees

Or clouds on a rainy day.

Several battles were lost,

And De'ang villages were occupied by the enemy.

我族见此军心散，
各路谣传人心惶。
于是连夜拾财物，
纷纷逃亡向永昌。
楚雄昌宁由此失，
从此我族背井乡。

人们带着己财物，
纷纷踏上逃亡路。
白米就让白马驮，
谷子花马来背负。
逃亡大军浩荡荡，
走出城镇离村庄。
就像惊飞之群鸟，
亦如众蚁搬家忙。
人们穿过大森林，
越过峻岭与高山。
野林茅地走成路，
终于到达至永昌。
才见永昌我德昂，
大家齐声便呼喊：
"赶快走啊赶快逃，

漫漫坎坷迁徙路
A Long and Arduous Journey of Migration

The De'ang soldiers lost the will to fight,

Frightened by all kinds of rumors.

So they gathered their supplies at night,

And fled to Yongchang,

Abandoning Changning and Chuxiong

And leaving our homelands forever.

People carried their belongings

And started their journey of exile.

White rice was carried by white horses,

And rice with husks by colored horses.

An army of fugitives

Fled the towns and villages.

They were just like a flock of startled birds

Or ants moving their home busily.

They went through forests

And climbed over high mountains.

So much walking created paths in the fields,

And they finally reached Yongchang.

The moment they saw the De'ang residents there,

They shouted in chorus,

"Run away! Run away fast!

敌人就在后追赶。
傣汉联军多如蜂,
很快追杀至永昌。
区区弹丸永昌地,
怎与敌军来相抗。
如果此时还不走,
迟早头落把命丧。
赶快收拾来逃命,
敌军实在太凶蛮。"
永昌德昂闻此语,
亦如惊弓飞鸟然。
个个争先又恐后,
加入人群来逃难。
最后一群走得迟,
紧赶大队赶不上。
前面人们皆担忧,
后来族人不识路。
于是边走边用刀,
砍断芭蕉做路标。
待后来人赶到后,
芭蕉已然新叶出。
路标一失人茫然,

漫漫坎坷迁徙路
A Long and Arduous Journey of Migration

The enemy are pursuing us.

The Dai and Han troops are as numerous as bees.

They will soon be in Yongchang.

Yongchang city is so small,

How can it resist the enemy?

If you don't flee now,

Soon you will lose your life.

Pack up and run now,

For the enemy is too fierce."

When the De'ang people in Yongchang heard this,

They were also like startled birds.

Everyone was terrified

And joined the crowds escaping in haste.

The last group left late

And couldn't catch up with the others.

People fleeing ahead were afraid

That they would be lost.

So on their way

They chopped down banana trees as road signs.

But when the people following them arrived,

New banana shoots and leaves had grown.

Because the signs were lost,

达古达楞格莱标 // Da-gu Da-leng Gelaibiao

不知逃亡向何方。

只好留在潞江坝,

辟地而居至如今。

因此我族德昂语,

将之称为"德昂隔①"。

再说前面我德昂,

一路逃亡至怒江。

只见水流深且急,

无法渡江哭爹娘。

有多族人被敌军,

赶入江中溺水亡。

所幸能飞数勇士,

将人一一背过江。

他们首先将老弱,

以及妇孺先背渡。

暂时安置在勐龙②,

再返江边渡余部。

如此耗时至数月,

才将余人尽背渡。

渡过怒江我族人,

---

① 德昂隔:德昂语,意为来迟了、落伍掉队的人。
② 勐龙:地名,今保山市龙陵县。亦称"弄令",意为爷爷、祖祖居住的地方。

漫漫坎坷迁徙路
A Long and Arduous Journey of Migration

The ones who followed didn't know where to go.

They had to stop in Lujiangba,

And have stayed there until today.

So the De'ang word for that group

Is "De'angge①".

When these people running ahead

Reached the Nujiang River,

They found the water was too deep and swift

To cross and began to cry.

Many De'ang people were driven into the river

By the enemy and drowned.

Fortunately, the warriors who could fly

Carried people across the river.

They first carried the old and the weak,

And then the women and children.

They temporarily settled them in Menglong②,

And returned to the river to carry the rest.

It took months

Before all were carried across the river.

The late-comers joined the groups

---

① De'angge: It means "people lagging behind".
② Menglong: It's today's Longling County, Baoshan City. It's also called "Nongling", meaning "the place where grandfathers and great grandfathers used to live".

终于勐龙相汇合。
至今德昂犹传诵，
时人励志之名言：
"智慧力胜大力士，
团结能挫万千军。"

二

话说能飞诸勇士，
先将老幼勐龙置。
然后返回怒江边，
两岸来回渡群滞。
可是人数实在多，
耗时数月犹未尽。
人们久滞在两岸，
随身食物渐告罄。
许多老弱成饿殍，
棚漏衣烂风雨侵。
处处哀号神鬼泣，
人间莫过此惨境。
诸位勇士来回飞，
背人背物身疲惫。

漫漫坎坷迁徙路
A Long and Arduous Journey of Migration

Who had come and settled there first.

Up to today,

Inspirational sayings of that time are remembered:

"Wisdom is more powerful than strength,

Solidarity can defeat thousands of troops."

II

The mighty warriors who could fly

Carried and settled the old and the weak in Menglong.

Then they went back and forth to carry

The other people who were still stranded.

But there were so many of them

That it took months to carry all across the river.

People were stranded on the river banks,

And their food soon ran out.

Many old and weak people died of hunger

And lack of protection from wind and rain.

Wailing cries were heard everywhere.

There was no place more miserable than this.

The mighty warriors flew back and forth,

Exhausted from carrying so many people and things.

终将人货渐渡尽,

得于勐龙相集汇。

我族于此得喘息,

野菜野果暂充饥。

德昂凭借聪明慧,

建房开荒又种地。

数年之后大变样,

生活境况得改良。

八方失散之族人,

亦渐来归话沧桑。

由于人口渐渐多,

勐龙地狭不能容。

于是成群又结队,

辗转迁徙踏边陲。

有的先行到勐焕①,

这里坝宽地肥美。

于是就在此地带,

处处建村又立寨。

帕底② 弄转与弄喊,

拱母芒牙及芒棒。

---

① 勐焕:地名,今德宏州首府芒市,意为金鸡报晓的地方。
② 帕底、弄转、弄喊、拱母、芒牙、芒棒:芒市六个傣族村寨的名称。据说,包括此六个村寨在内的芒市众多村寨,最初皆为德昂族所建,德昂族撤离后,由傣族所据。

漫漫坎坷迁徙路
A Long and Arduous Journey of Migration

Finally they carried all of them across the river,

And joined those already in Menglong.

The De'ang ancestors could at last have a rest there,

With wild fruits and vegetables as their food.

Depending on their wisdom, the De'ang people

Built houses and cultivated fields.

A few years later great changes had taken place

And their life had improved a lot.

The De'ang people who wandered in different places

Gradually came and told their stories.

As the population grew larger,

Menglong became too narrow of a place.

So they moved again in groups

To remote border areas.

Some going ahead came to a place named Menghuan[①],

Where the plains were wide and the fields were fertile.

So in this area,

They built many villages such as

---

① Menghuan: It's another name for Mangshi, capital city of Dehong Prefecture. It means "a place where the golden rooster first crows at dawn".

如此众多村与寨,

皆为此时我族建。

有的迁徙至勐棉①,

同样建立村与寨。

此时勐棉德昂首,

乃是亲生两兄弟。

哥哥与弟来商议,

决定哥哥留勐棉。

弟弟率部往勐底②,

建村立寨树根基。

故此又将此两地,

称为勐兄与勐弟。

时有一部称为"腊③",

亦出勐龙觅地栖。

彼之先祖与我祖,

本是同胞之兄弟。

因自天国下凡迟,

故而得此"腊"称谓。

彼族至一肥美地,

建村立寨辟地居

---

① 勐棉:地名,即今天的保山市腾冲市。
② 勐底:地名,即今天的德宏州梁河县。
③ 腊:据说为德昂族的一支,相传其先祖同德昂族其他先祖从天国下凡的时候,因为来得太迟,故称"腊"。

A Long and Arduous Journey of Migration

Padi①, Nongzhuan, Nonghan,

Gongmu, Mangya and Mangbang.

So many villages

Were all built by our ancestors during that period.

Some others migrated to Mengmian②

And established villages there, too.

The two De'ang leaders in Mengmian at that time

Were blood brothers.

The two brothers had a talk and decided

That the elder brother would stay in Mengmian

While the younger brother lead a group to Mengdi③,

Where they established many villages.

So people also called these two places

Elder Brother's Kingdom and Younger Brother's Kingdom.

In the same period, there was a tribe named La④,

Which also left Menglong for a better place.

Their ancestors and our ancestors

---

① Padi, Nongzhuan, Nonghan, Gongmu, Mangya, Mangbang: They are names of six Dai villages in Mangshi. It's said that many villages in Mangshi, including these, were originally built by the De'ang people, and after the De'ang people evacuated, they were occupied by the Dai people.
② Mengmian: It is a place located in Tengchong County, Baoshan City.
③ Mengdi: It is a place located in Lianghe County in Dehong Prefecture.
④ La: It is said to be a branch of the De'ang people. According to legend, when their ancestors descended from heaven with other ancestors of the De'ang people, they came too late and therefore they were called "La".

因之此地称勐腊①,

至今名称未曾易。

是时勐宛盏达②等,

亦多村寨我族立。

时于勐宛德昂中,

有一勇妇脱颖出。

佩刀大如芭蕉叶,

空中来去能飞舞。

彼即德昂之女王,

无所畏惧称英武。

居于崃允③傲四方,

麾下之士皆翘楚。

---

① 勐腊:地名,即今天的德宏州盈江县,意为腊人居住的地方。
② 勐宛、盏达:勐宛,地名,即今天的德宏州陇川县,意为太阳初升就能照到的地方;盏达,地名,即今天德宏州盈江县大江江西一带的区域。
③ 崃允:古地名,在今天的德宏州陇川境内,具体地点不详。据说,"允"为德昂女王的名字,"崃允"意为女王居住的地方。

漫漫坎坷迁徙路
A Long and Arduous Journey of Migration

Were brothers sharing the same father and mother.

As their ancestors came from heaven to earth late,

He was called La.

The tribe found a fertile land

And built houses and established villages there.

So that place was called Mengla①,

A name that is still in use today.

Other villages, such as Mengwan and Zhanda②,

Were also built by the De'ang people of that time.

Among the De'ang people in Mengwan,

There was a brave outstanding woman,

Who had a saber as big as a banana leaf,

And could fly back and forth in the air.

She was the queen of the De'ang people

And a valiant heroine fearing of nothing.

She lived in Laiyun③ and was very famous,

Because her warriors were among the best.

---

① Mengla: It is a place located in Yingjiang County in Dehong Prefecture and it means "the place where the La tribe used to live".

② Mengwan, Zhanda: They are the names of two places. Mengwan is located in Longchuan County in Dehong Prefecture and it means the first place the sun shines on as soon as it rises. Zhanda is located to the west of the Yingjiang River in Yingjiang County, Dehong Prefecture.

③ Laiyun: It's an ancient place located somewhere in today's Longchuan County, Dehong Prefecture. It is said that "Yun" is the name of the queen of a De'ang tribe, and "Laiyun" means "the place where the queen used to live".

达古达楞格莱标 // Da-gu Da-leng Gelaibiao

彼时德昂俱勇敢，
聪明者多亦非常。
却如盘中散沙聚，
各怀私心多骄蛮。
曾尚居于勐龙时，
不受法制称霸王。
汉民才把谷子收，
彼即用马强驮走。
汉族苞谷方成熟，
彼即霸占为己有。
汉民含泪谓彼言，
此是我粮莫抢走。
彼答"此山皆属我，
你若不种我不收。
如今你既把粮种，
自然我族全纳受"。
当时德昂我族人，
倚己势众逞骄横。
当时只因汉人少，
只能忍气又吞声。
如此经过有数年，

漫漫坎坷迁徙路
A Long and Arduous Journey of Migration

In those days, the De'ang people were brave,

And many were wise and talented.

But just like loose sand lacking cohesiveness,

Everyone was barbaric and selfish.

When they lived in Menglong,

They were living like lawless tyrants.

No sooner had the Han people harvested their rice

Than they took it away on horseback.

Just as the Han people's corns had ripened,

They seized it as their own.

With tears in their eyes the Han people said,

That grain was mine and should not be taken.

Their reply was, "This mountain belongs to us.

We won't take it if you don't plant it.

Now that you have grown crops here,

Naturally they should belong to me."

In those days our De'ang ancestors

Were arrogant because they were many,

And the Han people were few,

Thus the Han people had to submit to humiliation.

Years passed,

汉族终于无可忍。
于是偷偷至永昌，
搬来汉兵兴讨伐。
由于汉兵来得少，
交战未几遂败逃。
汉军经此一役后，
又是羞愧又气恼。
于是联络傣族军，
共将德昂来伐讨。
双方几经阵仗后，
彼此伤亡皆惨重。
胜负一时难分明，
联军遂撤暂休兵。

不久战端再度开，
汉傣联军卷土来。
联军汹汹声势大，
兵将如云神鬼哀。
他们扬言将德昂，
一举消灭偿宿债。
勐龙德昂闻讯后，
将族老幼深山藏。

漫漫坎坷迁徙路
A Long and Arduous Journey of Migration

The Han people could not bear it any more.

So they secretly went to Yongchang

And asked the Han troops to carry out a crusade.

Because the Han army was not strong enough,

They lost the battle very quickly.

After the battle,

The Han soldiers felt ashamed and angry.

So they requested help from the Dai army,

And together they attacked the De'ang people.

After several battles,

Both sides suffered heavy losses.

The war ended in a stalemate

And the allies withdrew their troops.

But soon the battle started again.

The Han and Dai armies made a comeback.

They were so powerful and overwhelming

That even ghosts felt frightened.

They threatened to take revenge on the De'ang people

And would wipe them out in one stroke.

When the De'ang people in Menglong heard it,

They hid the old and the young in the mountains.

其余只要能握刀，
男女全都上战场。
双方反复相厮杀，
血流成河日月暗。
最后德昂抵不住，
便向勐焕来逃亡。
当时勐焕德昂首，
居于帕底来运筹。
他将勐龙与勐焕，
两处人马合一流。
汉傣联军旋即至，
双方鏖战鬼神愁。
联军越战人越多，
德昂眼看不能守。
我族能人与勇士，
尽皆战死尸无收。
头人无奈率残部，
勐龙方向而溃走。
联军且追且扬言，
要赶德昂下怒江。
德昂残部似惊鸟，
偃旗逃遁入深山。

And the other men and women all joined the battle,

So long as they were strong enough to carry a knife.

The two sides fought each other again and again,

The sun darkened and blood flowed like rivers.

At last the De'ang people couldn't resist any longer

And fled to Menghuan.

The chief of Menghuan at the time

Directed the war from Padi, where he lived.

He combined the forces

Of Menglong and Menghuan.

The Han and Dai army soon arrived,

And the two sides were again at war.

The enemy was being continuously reinforced,

And the De'ang troops were fighting a losing battle.

The mighty De'ang men were all killed,

And their bodies were scattered over the battlefield.

The chief of the De'ang troops had no choice

But to flee toward Menglong.

The allied forces chased them and vowed

To push them into the Nujiang River.

Like frightened birds, the remnants of the De'ang troops

Escaped into the mountains, where they picked up

彼携藏山之老幼，
沿江逃向崃弄方。

联军获胜气如虹，
挥师又将勐棉攻。
勐棉城墙岩石筑，
荆棘生于岩缝中。
荆藤顺着岩石爬，
满布城墙四围中。
城墙之外又种满，
围绕城池荆棘丛。
就是善攀之猿猴，
不敢越此荆棘塘。
联军乍到不知机，
胜心切切往前冲。
可是数次把城攻，
皆因荆棘伤亡重。
久攻不下只好将，
城池围得水不通。
汉傣联军只得在，
城墙外面空徘徊。
德昂军士常瞅准，

漫漫坎坷迁徙路
A Long and Arduous Journey of Migration

The old and the young already hiding there

And fled along the river toward Lainong.

The allied forces won the war

And went on to attack Mengmian.

The city walls of Mengmian were built of stone,

And thorns grew out of the cracks.

The vines of the thorns crawled up the rocks

And covered the walls.

Outside the walls,

More thorns were planted around the city.

Even monkeys, good at climbing,

Dared not climb over those thorny walls.

At first, not knowing this,

The allied forces rushed toward the city walls.

They attacked the city several times,

But suffered heavy casualties from the thorns.

Unable to conquer the city in a short time,

The Han and Dai troops

Surrounded the city tightly,

Waiting outside the city walls with nothing to do.

When the De'ang soldiers saw that

敌军防备松懈时,
潜出城外毙数敌,
复又撤归城池中。
如此相持时日久,
联军渐渐军心动。
汉傣兵卒人人惧,
敌袭犹似虎出笼。
联军首领遂传令,
大军撤离暂休兵。

勐棉之围得解后,
日久守备渐渐松。
此时汉军一谋臣,
破城妙计蕴胸中。
彼将妙计向上献,
自告奋勇入勐棉。
他将自身扮银匠,
于敌城中四处游。
表面且将买卖做,
日日银器细加工。
暗地天天将碎银,
偷偷撒向荆棘丛。

漫漫坎坷迁徙路
A Long and Arduous Journey of Migration

The enemy troops were not vigilant,

They went out of the town, killed a few,

And retreated inside the city walls.

This continued,

And the allied troops gradually lost confidence.

They were scared

By the surprise attacks of the De'ang troops.

So the commander of the allied forces gave the order

To temporarily withdraw the troops.

After the battle in Mengmian was won,

The De'ang soldiers relaxed themselves.

A counselor of the Han army

Came up with a good idea to conquer the city.

He offered his great plan to the commander

And volunteered to go into Mengmian.

He disguised himself as a silversmith

And wandered around the De'ang city.

Apparently, he was doing business

And made silver ornaments every day.

Secretly, however, he threw silver pieces

Into the thorn bushes every day.

达古达楞格莱标 // Da-gu Da-leng Gelaibiao

德昂人见荆丛中，
颇多碎银无主翁。
于是人人争相捡，
渐渐砍光荆棘蓬。
只顾捡银德昂人，
似乎忘此护城重。
银匠又将茅草种，
和泥制成数多丸。
无事就操篾弹弓[①]，
射入城墙岩缝中。
德昂人见皆笑彼，
笑他无聊笑他疯。
待到雨季来临后，
城墙遍生茅草丛。
及至秋冬茅草枯，
汉傣大军复来攻。
联军点燃茅草丛，
烈火转瞬毁荆屏。
继而火势更威猛，
旋即蔓延至城中。

---

① 篾弹弓：一种用竹子制作而成的弹弓，能弹射泥丸和石子。过去西南各少数民族都用它作为猎杀小型动物和飞禽的工具。

漫漫坎坷迁徙路
A Long and Arduous Journey of Migration

The De'ang people saw that there were

So many silver pieces free for the taking.

They cut down the thorns

And scrambled for the silver pieces.

Busy picking up the silver,

They forgot the function of the thorns as defense works.

The silversmith mixed cogon grass seeds with mud

And made many pellets, which, when he was free,

He shot into the cracks in the city walls

With his bamboo slingshot①.

The De'ang people laughed at him,

Saying he was foolish and crazy.

When the rainy season came,

The walls were covered with cogon grass.

When the grass withered in autumn and winter,

The Han and Dai army returned to attack.

They set fire to the grass,

And the fire destroyed the thorn walls instantly.

Then the fire got stronger

And spread into the city.

---

① Bamboo slingshot: A slingshot was made of bamboo that could shoot mud pellets and stones. In the past, various ethnic minorities in southwest China used it as a tool for hunting small animals and birds.

大小房屋成灰烬，
灾祸突临满城惊。
联军趁机破城入，
满城尽飘汉傣旌。

德昂失却勐棉城，
残部逃亡向勐底。
此时昆明之汉官，
又派大军往驰援。
汉傣联军势更盛，
乘胜追杀至勐底。
由于联军势力大，
勐底德昂力难撑。
且战且退至勐腊，
与此合兵共相抗。
无奈敌军实在强，
只好再退至勐宛。
勐腊勐宛与勐卯，
三地德昂遂联合。
勐宛女王为主帅，
与汉傣军来相抗。
彼时勐宛之女王，

漫漫坎坷迁徙路
A Long and Arduous Journey of Migration

The houses turned into ash, and the whole city

Was shocked by this sudden disaster.

The allies broke into the city,

And their flags flew in all the streets.

So the De'ang people lost Mengmian city

And fled to Mengdi.

At this time the Han chief of Kunming

Sent strong reinforcements to help.

So the allied army, now more powerful,

Followed the De'ang troops to Mengdi.

Because of the great power of the allies,

The De'ang people in Mengdi had to give up

And retreated further to Mengla,

Where they fought back with Mengla's soldiers.

But the enemy was so strong

That they had to retreat farther into Mengwan.

Then the united troops

Of Mengla, Mengwan and Mengmao,

With the queen of Mengwan as the general commander,

Fought the Han and Dai army.

The queen of Mengwan

力大勇武无能当。

长刀大似芭蕉叶,

以一当十敌胆寒。

两军鏖战称惨烈,

汉傣联军倍伤亡。

此时忽自缅甸方,

杀出一支汉傣军。

德昂军遭两面击,

不久溃败四散逃。

唯有德昂之女王,

率部顽抗不投降。

由于女王太勇武,

汉傣兵将无能当。

于是想出擒王计,

将"恒①"置彼必经路。

女王不知道路险,

双足中套遂被俘。

汉傣兵将使刀枪,

欲毙彼命无能伤。

只好将其沉水中,

石木镇压一命殇。

---

① 恒:一种过去德昂人用于捕猎野兽的工具。

漫漫坎坷迁徙路
A Long and Arduous Journey of Migration

Was strong and brave without equal.

Using a sword as big as a banana leaf,

She could pit herself against ten enemy soldiers.

The two armies fought bitterly,

And the Han and Dai army suffered heavy casualties.

Suddenly, another Han and Dai army

Arrived from Burma.

The De'ang troops were now attacked on both sides,

And were soon defeated and scattered.

Only the De'ang queen

Kept on fighting and refused to surrender.

Because the queen was so brave

The Han and Dai soldiers were no match for her.

They worked out a plan to capture the queen

By putting a trap in her way.

The queen didn't know the trick

And was captured with both feet trapped.

The Han and Dai soldiers tried every kind of weapon,

But they could not hurt the queen.

They had to drown her in the water,

With stones and wood logs dragging her down.

达古达楞格莱标 // Da-gu Da-leng Gelaibiao

呜呼一代豪杰女,

玉陨沙场羞儿男。

经此一役我德昂,

余属逃亡果敢①方。

汉军不久班师回,

傣族遂得主此邦。

此时芒牙与邦外,②

乃二仅存德昂寨。

傣族军队数度攻,

奈何两寨互依赖。

傣军如若攻芒牙,

邦外援兵必定来。

倘若先将邦外攻,

芒牙亦必援邦外。

傣军硬攻不能取,

只有使出离间计。

傣军遣自族长者,

往觐芒牙之头人。

献上白银及厚礼,

---

① 果敢:地名,位于今天缅甸的北部地区。
② 芒牙、邦外:芒牙,傣族村寨名,由今天的芒市轩岗乡所辖。相传过去由德昂族所建,后被傣族所占。邦外,位于今天的芒市三台山,由三台山乡所辖,今天仍然是德昂族聚居的村寨。

漫漫坎坷迁徙路
A Long and Arduous Journey of Migration

Alas! Shame on these men that a great woman warrior

Should be killed in that way.

After that battle,

The remnants of the De'ang troops fled to Kokang①.

Soon the Han army returned to their place,

And the Dai people took control of the De'ang areas.

At that time Mangya and Bangwai②

Were the only two De'ang villages left.

The Dai army attacked them several times,

But the two villages were interdependent.

If the Dai army attacked Mangya,

Bangwai would send troops to help.

If the Dai army attacked Bangwai,

Mangya would also send troops to help.

The Dai could not occupy the two villages by force,

So they resorted to sowing discord between them.

They sent their tribal chiefs as envoys

---

① Kokang: It's a place located in the northern part of Myanmar today.
② Mangya, Bangwai: Mangya is a Dai village under the jurisdiction of Xuangang Township in Mangshi City, Dehong Prefecture. According to legend, it was built by De'ang people in the past, and later occupied by Dai people. Bangwai is a village under the jurisdiction of Santaishan Township in Mangshi City, Dehong Prefecture. Today there is still a village inhabited by De'ang people.

软言悦彼求议和。
情愿甘做芒牙属,
互不相犯息干戈。
芒牙头人闻说后,
满心欢喜遂议和。
傣军使者乘此机,
将谗言进行离间:
"我听邦外头人言,
说大王您没本事。
过去傣军相攻伐,
全靠邦外来相助。
若无邦外施援手,
大王定成落群鼠。"
芒牙头人闻此言,
暗自忿忿寻报复。
自讨今有傣军护,
何需邦外来相顾。
傣军又以相同法,
遣使邦外行离间。
邦外芒牙两寨首,
内心遂互生忿怨。
傣军得见战机熟,

漫漫坎坷迁徙路
A Long and Arduous Journey of Migration

To visit the De'ang leader of Mangya.

They gave him a lot of silver and other gifts,

And coaxed him into a peace settlement.

They said they would like to be ruled by Mangya

And stop fighting each other.

When the head of Mangya heard this,

He was happy and so they signed a peace treaty.

The envoys of the Dai army

Went on to irritate him:

"I hear the chief of Bangwai

Say that Your Majesty is not competent at all,

And when the Dai army attacked your village,

Your victory depended on his help.

If there was no help from him,

Your Majesty would have lost the battle, like a rat."

When the head of Mangya heard this,

He got angry and decided to take revenge,

Thinking that he now had the Dai army's protection

And needed no help from others.

The Dai army used the same strategy

On the chief of Bangwai.

The heads of two villages

遽然兴兵攻邦外。

邦外独力难支撑,

损兵折将乱纷纷。

此时邦外之头人,

犹盼芒牙来援增。

可是战余十数卒,

不见芒牙来一人。

邦外头人无奈何,

带领数人户育①逃。

不料此时户育寨,

早已空空无一人。

转身又投弄转去,

哪知弄转人亦空。

只好暂于弄转奘②,

短暂休息避敌锋。

此时邦外之头人,

悲愤交集失声恸。

愤然挥刀向房柱,

柱遂被砍数寸深。

据说弄转奘房内,

---

① 户育：傣族村寨名，由今天的芒市风平镇所辖。相传过去由德昂族所建，后被傣族所占。

② 弄转奘：弄转，傣族村寨名，由今天的芒市风平镇所辖，相传过去由德昂族所建，后被傣族所占。"奘"，即佛寺。弄转奘，就是弄转寨子的佛寺。

漫漫坎坷迁徙路
A Long and Arduous Journey of Migration

Now bore resentment towards each other.

The Dai army seized the opportunity

To launch a sudden attack on Bangwai.

Without help from Mangya,

Bangwai suffered heavy losses.

But the chief of Bangwai

Still expected help from Mangya.

Yet even when they had only a dozen soldiers left,

No one from Mangya came to their rescue.

Helpless, he fled to Huyu[①],

Followed by only a few people.

To his surprise,

Huyu village was already empty.

He turned around and escaped to Nongzhuan,

Only to find that it was also empty.

He had to stay at the Nongzhuan Temple[②]

For a short rest to escape the enemy.

Now the head of Bangwai cried out loud,

---

① Huyu: It's a Dai village under the jurisdiction of Fengping Town in Mangshi. According to legend, it was built by De'ang people in the past, and later occupied by Dai people.

② Nongzhuan Temple: Nongzhuan is a Dai village under the jurisdiction of Fengping Town, Mangshi. According to legend, it was built by De'ang people in the past, and later occupied by Dai people.

至今柱留此刀痕。
随后彼等沿怒江,
辗转逃亡缅甸方。

傣军剿灭邦外后,
立即毁约袭芒牙。
芒牙大意疏守备,
猝不及防一击溃。
兵将大部皆战死,
老弱妇孺成玉碎。
此时头人醒已迟,
后悔未曾援邦外。
时彼不知邦外首,
已往缅甸去逃亡。
遂骑快马要去找,
邦外头人来帮忙。
不料却于必经路,
落入陷阱被敌擒。

A Long and Arduous Journey of Migration

Feeling both sad and angry.

In a burst of temper, he slashed a pillar of the temple

With his sword, making a cut several inches deep.

Legend has it that on that pillar of the temple in Nongzhuan,

One can still see the cut left by the sword.

Then he and his men fled to Burma

Along the Nujiang River,

After the Dai army took Bangwai,

They tore the treaty up at once and attacked Mangya.

Mangya was careless about its defense

And lost the battle in no time.

Most of the soldiers and generals died in the battle,

So did the old, the weak, women and children.

By now the chief realized his mistake, but it was too late.

He regretted not having helped Bangwai.

He didn't know

That the chief of Bangwai had fled to Burma.

So he got on a horse

And hurried to Bangwai's chief for help,

But on the way, he fell into a trap

And got caught by the enemy.

达古达楞格莱标 // Da-gu Da-leng Gelaibiao

傣首下令将他斩,
刀砍矛戳不能伤。
于是傣军遂将其,
缚于大树柴堆上。
付之一炬大火燃,
我族英烈一命殇。

由于往昔多作恶,
外凌他族内不睦。
自私自利不修德,
不敬尊长及父母。
凡此种种恶劣行,
惹得人神齐发怒。
以致能人皆死尽,
举族倍尝流离苦。
丧失家园四处漂,
致成人口最少族。
所幸汉傣之头人,
胸中尚存慈悯心。
没将我族赶杀尽,
德昂方能衍于今。
故劝后辈我儿孙,

漫漫坎坷迁徙路
A Long and Arduous Journey of Migration

The Dai chief ordered him to be beheaded,

But swords and spears could not harm him.

So the Dai army bundled him up, tied him to a big tree

With a pile of firewood under it,

And set fire to it.

Thus a De'ang people's hero lost his life.

Because of all the evil deeds they had done,

While troubled with internal conflicts,

The De'ang people bullied other ethnic groups.

Selfish and immoral,

They did not respect their elders or parents.

All these misdeeds angered both gods and humans,

So that many capable people had died,

And the whole De'ang people suffered from displacement.

Losing their homes and roaming around,

They became the least populated group.

Fortunately, the chiefs of the Han and Dai people

Were kind and showed mercy to them.

They didn't slaughter all of the De'ang people,

So that our ethnic group could survive and multiply.

Here is advice for all the De'ang people:

莫随前人恶劣行。
外睦他族内修德,
凡所到处互相亲。

三

达古达楞传至今,
历史教训记于心。
昔因我族太横骄,
才失家园四处飘。
逃亡道路艰又险,
怒江水急风雨潇。
再说当年我德昂,
逃亡路断怒江哮。
傣汉联军曾扬言,
要将德昂喂波涛。
许多乡亲及父老,
皆被溺毙满江漂。

时有勐龙德昂人,
沿江往下去逃生。
途中峭岩挡去路,

漫漫坎坷迁徙路
A Long and Arduous Journey of Migration

Do not follow the misdeeds of our predecessors,

But cultivate our virtues, live in peace with others,

And be kind to others wherever we go.

III

As we sing the De'ang old song *Da-gu Da-leng* today,

We should learn from the lessons of history:

Because our ancestors were too arrogant,

They lost their homelands and fled in all directions.

Escaping was difficult and dangerous, and they had to face

The treacherous Nujiang River, strong winds and rain.

Our De'ang ancestors were blocked

By the rumbling river on their road of exile.

The Dai and Han allies threatened

To drown the De'ang people in the rolling waves.

Many De'ang folks

Were drowned and floated on the river.

There were the De'ang people from Menglong,

Who escaped along the river.

A steep cliff blocked them on the way,

达古达楞格莱标 // Da-gu Da-leng Gelaibiao

人人慌乱尽失神。
此时头人四处看,
寻找攀越峭岩方。
他见岩上枯树桩,
跃身抓住往上攀。
不料树老心已空,
连人带树落江中。
是时头人急生智,
紧紧抱住空心木。
随着汹涌之江水,
一路漂流至勐峡①。
江水将彼冲上岸,
侥幸奇迹得生还。
从此头人倍珍惜,
救命空心老木桩。
一日头人入深山,
猎获一头山羚羊。
他将羊皮晒干后,
紧紧绷于木两头。
如此便是我德昂,
独有水鼓之来由。

---

① 勐峡:地名,位于今天的缅甸北部地区,靠近峡弄的一个小地方。

A Long and Arduous Journey of Migration

And everyone lost his mind in confusion, not knowing what to do.

The chief looked around

For a way to climb over the steep cliff.

He saw a dead tree trunk on the cliff

And jumped up to grasp it.

But the old tree was hollow and rotten

And he fell into the river with the tree.

He clung to the trunk tightly

In a desperate effort to survive.

Floating on the rushing water,

He drifted all the way to Menglai[①].

The water washed him ashore,

And fortunately and miraculously, he survived.

Since then the chief cherished the hollow tree trunk

That had saved his life.

One day he went deep into the mountains

And caught an antelope.

He dried its skin

And tightened it to both ends of the trunk.

That is how the water drum came into being

And became unique to the De'ang people.

---

① Menglai: It is a small place near Lainong, located in the northern part of Myanmar.

达古达楞格莱标 // Da-gu Da-leng Gelaibiao

头人制成水鼓后,

敲得鼓声咚咚扬。

四处逃散德昂人,

得闻鼓声咚咚响。

知是头人之召唤,

八方聚拢来相商。

结果众人意见同,

决定建寨并立勐①。

辛日伊始建阿瓦②,

逢申之日建崃弄。

阿瓦地处炎热坝,

欲解干渴无有茶。

崃弄茶山乏水田,

一年三次饥来煎。

因此每逢谷子熟,

两地粮茶互交换。

阿瓦崃弄两相亲,

相互往来联系紧。

故而远近皆称扬,

团结互助渐繁兴。

---

① 勐:德昂族和傣族共用的称谓。过去将一个民族或部落独立管辖的区域或小国称为"勐"。

② 阿瓦:地名,位于今天的缅甸境内,为今天缅甸的瓦城。

漫漫坎坷迁徙路
A Long and Arduous Journey of Migration

After the chief made the water drum,

He beat it hard and its sound spread far and wide.

De'ang people, who were scattered in different places,

Heard the drum and realized

It was the call of their chief.

So they came to meet for a discussion.

They decided to build new villages

And establish new kingdoms①.

Thus Awa② was founded on an auspicious day,

And Lainong, on another.

Awa was located in a hot valley,

Where there was no tea to quench thirst.

Lainong was located on a tea mountain with no paddy fields,

Where people were stricken by three famines a year.

So when the rice was harvested,

The people of Awa and Lainong exchanged food and tea.

They lived in harmony,

And were closely related to each other.

Praised far and near, they owed their prosperity

To solidarity and mutual assistance.

---

① Kingdom: The De'ang and the Dai people use the word "meng" for "kingdom". In the past, an area or small country under the independent jurisdiction of an ethnic group or tribe was referred to as "meng", meaning "kingdom".

② Awa: It is located in today's Mandalay.

阿瓦崃弄德昂情,
很快传至汉官庭。
汉官忧彼成祸患,
又因不了彼实情,
担心兴兵反不利,
于是决定相招抚。
汉官遂派人出使,
阿瓦崃弄传谕旨。
欲招丙地德昂民,
悉返昆明垂拱治。
不料只有少数人,
随同使节共回还。
及至昆明谒汉官,
官手指上对其言:
"宫殿顶拴大风筝,
无有人能取其下。
尔等谁能取将来,
德昂便是吾皇民。
并给尔等颁印信,
赐予尔等姓与名。"
众皆顺指往上看,

漫漫坎坷迁徙路
A Long and Arduous Journey of Migration

The news of the good relationship between the two De'ang kingdoms

Was soon spread to the Han palace.

The Han governor worried that they would become a threat,

But he knew little about them.

Fearing that attacking them might cause disorder,

He decided to befriend them.

He sent envoys to Awa and Lainong

To deliver his official order to bring

The De'ang people of both places

Back to Kunming to enjoy peace.

But only a few De'ang people

Went with the envoys to Kunming.

When they arrived and visited the governor,

He pointed at the sky and said,

"A big kite is tied to the roof of the palace,

But no one can take it down.

If any of you can take the kite down,

The De'ang people will be subjects of the Han Emperor.

I will grant you an imperial seal

And bestow Han surnames on you."

Everybody looked up,

个个惊呼齐声叹。

只见风筝足三丈,

呼呼哧哧空中飘。

宫殿之顶高入云,

若非神人谁能攀。

不料在场德昂人,

其中头人确有能。

只见他于转眼间,

攀上殿顶取风筝。

取下风筝拽着绳,

校场数圈来回奔。

众人目睹此情景,

惊得呆愣尽失神。

汉官不住对头人,

"力大、力大"赞连声。

从此汉族见德昂,

便呼"力大"为其名。

在场傣族见此情,

手指头人连声呼:

"布龙转浪洪嘎沙①",

---

① 布龙转浪洪嘎沙——傣语。"布龙"是被水冲走的意思。整句意为:被怒江水冲走了的人。

And all sighed in astonishment.

The kite was ten meters long,

And it was flying in the air.

The roof of the palace rose into the clouds.

Only a man with magic power could climb that high.

Among the De'ang people present, however,

There was one man that could do it, the chief.

In the twinkling of an eye,

He climbed to the top and got the kite.

Taking down the kite and pulling the rope,

He ran several laps around the drill ground.

When the audience saw this,

They were extremely astonished.

The governor repeatedly praised the De'ang chief

"Strong! Strong!"

From then on, the Han people

Called the De'ang people "Strong" when they saw them.

The Dai people present saw this and pointed their fingers

At the De'ang chief and shouted,

"Bulong zhuan lang hong ga sha!"[①]

---

① Bulong zhuan lang hong ga sha: It is a sentence in the Dai language. "Bulong" means "being washed away by water". The whole sentence means "people washed away by the Nujiang River".

此言傣族遂传遍。
从此傣族见德昂，
便呼德昂为"布龙"。
汉语"布龙"讲不清，
日后遂成"崩龙"名。

"力大"取下风筝后，
汉官对其礼遇厚。
又与"力大"来商量，
欲其返招余部归。
"力大"诚对汉官言，
非是余部不愿归。
只因人人皆惧怕，
汉傣联军之神威。
如若只凭一面言，
诚难取信何相随？
汉官听罢"力大"语，
暗想此话亦有理。
于是即刻往京城，
一五一十奏皇帝。
皇帝闻奏龙颜喜，
将昔因缘对其语：

The words spread among the Dai people.

From then on, when the Dai people saw the De'ang people,

They called them "Bulong".

The Chinese word for "Bulong" was mispronounced

And gradually became "Benglong".

When the man "Strong" took down the kite,

The Han governor treated him courteously.

He talked with "Strong", hoping that he would

Go back and bring the rest of the De'ang people to be his subjects.

"Strong" told the governor the truth,

That his people would like to follow him,

But they were all afraid of

The power of the Han and Dai allied army.

A one-sided promise was hard to win trust.

Who would dare follow me?

The governor thought

That "Strong" was right.

He went immediately to the capital

And told the emperor about it.

The emperor was pleased to hear it

And told him the story of a marriage:

"前朝之时我先帝,
有妹年长无人娶。
后被德昂娶为妻,
故彼实为汉皇婿。
无论彼族何处去,
都不应将彼忘记。"
皇帝语罢即命人,
刻成印章相赐予。
印章上刻"崩龙记",
至今尚存在阿瓦。
汉族即从此时起,
将我德昂称"崩龙"。

汉官返回昆明后,
即刻宣召德昂首。
将此印信赐予彼,
又将皇帝龙言递:
"德昂乃是我臣民,
中华子孙无有疑。
今后无论居何处,
如此根本要牢记。"
我族头人受印已,

"The last emperor, my father, had a sister,

But no one came to propose to her when she grew up.

Later she was married to a De'ang man,

Who became the Han emperor's son-in-law.

Thus wherever the De'ang people have gone,

They will not be forgotten."

With that, the emperor gave an order

To make a seal for the De'ang people

And to inscribe the words "Benglong Seal" on it.

The seal is now in Awa.

From then on, the Han people

Called the De'ang people "Benglong".

After the Han governor returned to Kunming,

He immediately summoned the De'ang chief

And gave him the seal.

He then conveyed the emperor's message to him:

"The De'ang people are the Han emperor's subjects,

And undoubtedly a part of the Chinese nation.

No matter where you live in the future,

This is the most important thing to remember."

The De'ang chief accepted the seal

悲欣交集发誓语：
"德昂从前太骄蛮，
才被他族四处赶。
如今我等改前非，
安分守己不相欺。
吾乃汉皇之兄弟，
如此历史当牢记。"

四

日月轮转草木新，
斗转星移几春秋。
自从德昂自中国，
一路逃亡至崃弄。
安门立户建村寨，
转瞬已历经数代。
彼以种茶为生计，
家家户户渐富裕。
那时崃弄之德昂，
果达玛教无崇尚。
人人只信鬼与神，
恶习坚厚乏友善。

And felt both sad and happy, saying,

"We De'ang people have been so arrogant

That we've been driven about by others.

From now on we will mend our ways,

Abide by the rules and not bully others.

We are brothers of the emperor

And will keep this historical moment in mind."

IV

Several years had passed

And the world went on as usual.

It was several generations

Since the De'ang ancestors left China

And escaped all the way to Lainong

And built houses and villages there.

They made a living by growing tea,

And every family was becoming wealthy.

At that time the De'ang people in Lainong

Did not believe in Buddhism.

Everyone believed only in ghosts

And became vicious and unkind to others.

族内多诤不和睦，
殃祸频起多磨难。
彼时匪盗竞猖獗，
常有村寨遭掠劫。
杀人纵火无不为，
抢尽财物踪影绝。
我民不堪劫掠苦，
齐向西面头人诉。
西面头人不理睬，
又往东面头人处。
东面头人亦推诿，
直言无力来相护。
彼等不愿为小民，
招惹匪盗与相忤。
头人家亲因势强，
匪盗亦不相掠掳。
唯我德昂之小民，
仰问苍天谁相怙？
无奈只好又一次，
弃家逃往山深处。
可是深山多险恶，
瘴气恶鬼常相顾。

漫漫坎坷迁徙路
A Long and Arduous Journey of Migration

Even among themselves there was fighting.

There were frequent disasters and suffering.

In those days banditry was rampant,

And villages were often looted.

They did everything from killing to arson.

They robbed people of all they had and ran away.

Our people couldn't bear it any longer

And reported it to the chief in the west,

Who just ignored their complaints.

They had to turn to the chief in the east,

Who also wanted to stay out of it,

Saying he was powerless to help them.

The two chiefs did not want to provoke the bandits

By protecting the common people's interests.

Anyway, the chiefs' relatives were powerful

And the bandits dared not rob them.

Only the common De'ang people

Had no one to protect them.

Again, they had to abandon their homes

And flee into the mountains

Where they had to face many dangers

And cope with malaria and ghosts.

达古达楞格莱标 // Da-gu Da-leng Gelaibiao

大家只好跟循着,
象群足迹踏迁途。
不知走了多少天,
不知翻越几山谷。
人们终于来到了,
山清水秀之姐南①。
此地无有匪盗猖,
此地人多业兴旺。
此地适合我族居,
于是大家共相商。
决定携礼去拜访,
姐南头人乞相容。
不料见了头人后,
彼怀轻慢开口言:
"姐南三万八千寨,
各寨各有三万户。
麻雀归巢也迷路,
黄牛难觅己住处。
出门挑水的姑娘,
归时也会迷门户。
我们的水不够喝,

---

① 姐南:地名,位于今天缅甸北部,靠近中国瑞丽市的一个区域。

漫漫坎坷迁徙路
A Long and Arduous Journey of Migration

They had to follow a herd of elephants

On their migration.

They didn't know how many days they had walked

Or how many mountains and valleys they had crossed

Before they finally arrived in Jienan①,

A place of picturesque scenery,

Where people enjoyed a prosperous life,

Without thieves or bandits to harass them.

It was a suitable place for the De'ang people.

So they had a good discussion

And decided to visit the chief of Jienan,

Give him some gifts and ask him

For permission to settle down there.

But the chief spoke arrogantly,

"There are thirty-eight thousand villages in Jienan.

In each village there are thirty thousand households.

A sparrow may get lost when it returns to its nest,

And a cow cannot find its way home.

A girl who goes out to fetch water

May lose her way when she returns.

We have neither enough water to drink,

---

① Jienan: It's a place located in the northern part of Myanmar and it is near Ruili City, Dehong Prefecture.

我们的地不够住。
尔非贤玉之兄长,
亦非勐广兄弟属。①
此地无有你喝水,
亦无少地与你住。"
听罢头人之冷语,
无奈再次踏迁途。
众人继续往北走,
历尽千辛和万苦。
最后终于来到了,
芒市坝尾遮放头。
这里山高坝又平,
土地肥沃宜人居。
所幸汉傣之衙官,
胸怀宽厚相纳接。
从此我族于此地,
安寨落户好生息。
代代绵延至于今,
幸福美满庆安宁。

---

① 贤玉之兄长、勐广兄弟属:德昂族相传,龙公主将自己与太阳王子所生的五个金蛋抛落后,落在不同的区域,后自金蛋出生五个兄弟。落在贤玉的先出生,为兄长,落在勐广等地的为兄弟,他们都是德昂族的祖先。详见《太阳王子和龙公主》章。

漫漫坎坷迁徙路
A Long and Arduous Journey of Migration

Nor sufficient land to live on.

You are not descendants of the brother in Xianyu,

Nor are you from the Mengguang brother's branch.①

Here we don't have water to spare you,

Neither do we have any land for you."

Hearing the cold words of the chief,

They had no choice but to move on.

They kept going north,

Braving great difficulties and hardships.

And finally they arrived at a place

Between today's Mangshi plain and Zhefang.

Here there were high mountains and vast plains,

And the land was fertile and pleasant to live on.

Fortunately, the Han and the Dai officials here

Were generous enough to accept them.

So our people settled down.

Ever since then we have been living

And multiplying here

In happiness and peace.

---

① Xianyu; Mengguang: According to De'ang legend, the Dragon Princess had five golden eggs by the Sun Prince. She threw away the five eggs, which landed in different areas. Five sons were born from the golden eggs. The egg that fell on Xianyu gave birth to the eldest brother, and the other eggs falling on Mengguang and other places gave birth to the younger brothers. All the brothers were the ancestors of the De'ang people. More details can be found in "The Sun Prince and the Dragon Princess".

译后记

德昂族属于跨境民族，在历史上经历了多场战争，造成了人口的多次迁徙，与缅甸的德昂族、柬埔寨的高棉族同源。德昂族是中国人口较少民族之一，2010年全国人口普查数据为20556人，主要分布在云南省的德宏州和保山市，是云南特有民族之一，是新中国成立后，直接由原始社会过渡到社会主义社会的民族之一。

在长期的生产、生活实践中，德昂族靠着自己的勤劳智慧与创造能力，给人类留下了独具民族特色、丰富多彩、光辉灿烂的文化遗产。《达古达楞格莱标》是德昂族唯一一部创世神话史诗，2008年被列入第二批国家级非物质文化遗产保护名录。"达古达楞格莱标"的德昂语意为"最早的祖先传说"。

《达古达楞格莱标》全诗主要讲述天和地的形成、德昂人的来历、粮食和衣饰的由来、德昂人的迁徙之路4个方面的内容，由7个部分组成：序歌，天和地的由来，葫芦人的传说，茶树、粮种和衣饰的来历，太阳王子和龙公主，王宫斩龙，漫漫坎坷迁徙路。全诗长约 2200 行，对仗工整，每行都是 7 个字，采用了佛经中常使用的偈颂体，而这也是英译过程中只能保持原意、无法保持原文诗句语言特点的原因之一。

杨慧芳

Translator's Afterword

The De'ang people are a cross-border ethnic group. They have experienced many wars in history and undergone multiple migrations, and as a result share the same origin with the De'ang people in Myanmar and the Mon Khmer ethnic group in Cambodia. The De'ang people is one of the less populous ethnic groups in China. The 2010 national census data shows that their population at that time was 20556. The De'ang people mainly found in Dehong Prefecture and Baoshan City of Yunnan Province. The De'ang people is one of the ethnic groups indigenous only to Yunnan and one of the ethnic groups which moved directly from the primitive social stage into socialist society after the People's Republic of China was founded.

In the long course of production and labor, the wise, hard-working and innovative De'ang people created a unique, colorful and splendid cultural heritage with their own ethnic characteristics. Their only creation epic, *Da-gu Da-leng Gelaibiao*, composed of legends and stories, is one example. "Da-gu Da-leng Gelaibiao" is a De'ang term and it means "the legend of the earliest ancestors." In 2008, it was included

Translator's Afterword

on the second group of national intangible cultural heritage protection lists.

The entire epic mainly describes four aspects: the formation of the sky and the earth, the origin of the De'ang people, the origin of food and clothing, and the migration path of the De'ang people. It consists of seven parts: Prologue; The Origin of the Sky and the Earth; The Legend of the Gourd People; The Origin of Tea Trees, Grain Seeds and Clothes; The Sun Prince and the Dragon Princess; Killing the Dragon in the Royal Palace and A Long and Arduous Journey of Migration. The entire poem is composed of about 2200 lines with seven Chinese characters in each line. It adopts the chanting style commonly used in the Buddhist scriptures, which makes it so hard for the translator to reproduce the verse style of the Chinese original in the English language. Therefore, the translator has to focus on faithfulness to the inherent meaning.

Yang Huifang

译者简介

杨慧芳，云南师范大学外国语学院副教授。代表性译著为《景颇族文史画册》。课余时间和假期里喜欢从事社会公益工作，进行文学作品的翻译和文化交流工作，其中服务时间较长的机构项目为亚洲开发银行资助的联合国教科文组织广播剧创作、翻译和录制项目：《湄公河次区域山地民族地区艾滋病预防教育项目》。2004—2012年参与并完成了德宏景颇族、德宏傣族、西双版纳傣族、临沧佤族、凉山彝族等五个少数民族广播剧的英文翻译。

About the Translator

Yang Huifang is an associate professor of English in the School of Foreign Languages and Literature at Yunnan Normal University. Her representative translation publication is *Jingpo Historical & Cultural Photo Album* (Yunnan Nationality Publishing House, 2007). Her research interests focus on literary translation and cross-cultural communication. She worked in 2004−2012 as a coordinator, translator and interpreter on the ADB-funded UNESCO project *HIV/AIDS Prevention Education among Highland Peoples in Sub-Mekong Regions*, which consisted of five programs: *Jingpo Ethnic Program in Dehong, Dai Ethnic Program in Dehong, Dai Ethnic Program in Xishuangbanna, Wa Ethnic Program in Lincang and Yi Ethnic Program in Liangshan.*